Remember the Alamo!

Other Lone Star Journals

Get Along, Little Dogies: The Chisholm Trail
Diary of Hallie Lou Wells,
South Texas 1878

The Great Storm: The Hurricane
Diary of J. T. King,
Galveston, Texas 1900

The
Lone ★ *Star*
Journals

Book 3

Remember the Alamo!

The Runaway Scrape Diary of Belle Wood

Austin's Colony, Texas
1835—1836

Lisa Waller Rogers

Texas Tech University Press

This book is typeset in Galliard. The paper used in this book meets the minimum requirements of ANSI/NISO Z39.48-1992 (R1997).

Although her diary is based on historical events, Belle Woods is a fictional character.

Series design by Joan Osth
Printed in the United States of America

Library of Congress Cataloging-in-Publication Data
Rogers, Lisa Waller, 1955–
    Remember the Alamo! : the runaway scrape diary of Belle Wood,
    Austin's Colony, Texas, 1835-1836 / Lisa Waller Rogers.
        p.   cm. — (Lone star journals ; bk. 3)
Summary: A fourteen-year-old girl keeps a diary of events during the Texas Revolution, as her life changes from dances and picnics to flight from Santa Anna's army after the fall of the Alamo.
    ISBN 0-89672-497-2 (cloth : alk. paper)
[1. Frontier and pioneer life—Texas—Fiction. 2. Alamo (San Antonio, Tex.)—Siege, 1836—Fiction. 3. Texas—History—Revolution, 1835-1836—Fiction. 4. Diaries—Fiction.] I. Title.
PZ7.R63625 Re 2003
[Fic]—dc21

                                                        2003000602

03 04 05 06 07 08 09 10 11/9 8 7 6 5 4 3 2 1

Texas Tech University Press
Box 41037
Lubbock, Texas 79409-1037 USA
800.832.4042
ttup@ttu.edu
www.ttup.ttu.edu

With great love

To my turquoise grandmother,
Loise Belle Wood Waller
(1904–1997)
You were the life of the party.

The army will cross and we will meet the enemy. Some of us may be killed and must be killed; but, soldiers, remember the Alamo, the Alamo! the Alamo!

GENERAL SAM HOUSTON
addressing his Texian army
before the Battle of San Jacinto
April 19, 1836

Remember the Alamo!

Belle's Plantation World at Wood's Landing

The Wood Family

Belle—a teenage girl fond of family, friends, and horses, but not ghosts

Father—Belle's father, Squire Josiah Wood, a respected cotton planter and justice of the peace

Mother—Belle's mother, Madam Mary Wood, every inch a lady

Maurine—("Sister") Belle's boy-crazy older sister

Little Henrietta—Belle's younger sister

Mac—Belle's big brother

Grandma MacKenzie—("GM") Belle's grandmother

Visitors

Maggie O'Hara—Belle's best friend

The Baron de La Salle—a dashing French nobleman

Angus McCoy—a country farmer

Guy Morrison Bryan—a teenage boy who stays and
    studies with the Woods

Priscilla Pruitt—("Prissy") a teenage girl also lodging
    with the Woods

Flo—Prissy's maid

The Enslaved Servant Family

Milindy—Belle's maid

Uncle Peter—Milindy's father, who calls himself the "vice-president" of Wood's Landing

Aunty Rachel—Milindy's mother, a great cook, nurse, butcher, farmhand, cattle drover, midwife, and so forth

Moss—Milindy's big brother

Toby—Milindy's younger sister

Austin's Colony, Texas

1835–1836

Saturday, October 10, 1835

Almost midnight

Now this is creepy. I have no idea how I got home tonight.

The last thing I remember is when the sun went down. I was galloping like thunder across Bailey's Prairie on Beauty, my chestnut brown Morgan. I'd ridden out to see Maggie. It was growing darker and a cold rain had begun to fall. I wanted desperately to be home. But home was ten miles away, through a deep wood and across a river.

Then, lo and behold, the next thing I knew, I *was* at home. The first thing I noticed was the sound of our grandfather clock downstairs chiming ten o'clock. Ten o'clock? I sat straight up and looked around. I found myself here—in my own bed—and outside was total darkness. How'd I get here? Three hours before, I'd been in the saddle on Bailey's Prairie. What happened to those missing miles and minutes? Is Beauty all right?

My servants are running around me nervously.

As I write this, Aunty Rachel is plopped down beside me on the bed forcing cups of hot tea to my chilled lips. My teeth are chattering so badly I'm afraid I'll drip tea on this page. Milindy has stripped off my wet things, hung them up in front of the fire to dry, and slipped me into my warm dressing gown. Little Toby stands at the foot of my bed, holding a big-toothed comb, waiting for me to finish my tea so she can attack the knots in my mud-caked hair.

The three of them move about silently. They speak neither to me nor to one another, as if they shared some deep, dark secret about me too shameful to voice. What is my secret? What do these three people know about my three lost hours?

I do have one clue. When Aunty Rachel walked over to pour my tea, I heard her mutter something under her breath about me "messin' with that ghost."

That ghost? What ghost? Won't someone please tell me what happened tonight?

Aunty Rachel says, "No mo' questions." She's reaching for my diary and pen to take them away. She says I must sleep.

Sunday, October 11, 1835

At first light

Oh, my head! I can feel a bump on it the size of a goose's egg. And my poor body. Everything aches and throbs. Even my bruises have bruises. I wish I could remember what happened last night. Could I have fallen off my horse perhaps?

I hope General Cós does not plan to march his army through our plantation at Wood's Landing any time soon. Nothing short of a Mexican invasion could get me out of my feather bed today!

Late morning

Bits & pieces. That's still all I know about what happened last night. I just learned some of the newest pieces from my big sister, Maurine.

It was a few minutes past eight when she—not Milindy, as is usual—brought up my breakfast tray. My door was slightly ajar. "Good morning!" Maurine chirped, peeking in through the crack. I was sitting up in bed.

"Well, this is a surprise," I said, instantly suspicious. Sister, as I call her, has never ever served me breakfast in bed.

When Sister saw the bump on my forehead, her smile vanished. "Oh, Belle!" she cried. With great drama, she rushed to my side, depositing the tray on my lap. On it was a vase of little roses. I grabbed the vase as it tilted over, before water spilled everywhere.

Sister, oblivious to the mess she almost made, was

busily examining my forehead. "Why, it's all black and blue," she said, mashing the bump painfully with her thumb. When I cried, "Ouch!" she gave my bump a kiss.

She then bent in for such a close look that I could feel her breath on my face. "It's much worse than Milindy said it was!" she cooed.

Milindy—so, that was it. She'd been gossiping with Milindy. She hadn't come up to see me because she cared about my bump! She had come because she wanted a full account of my nighttime escapade. She'd talked Milindy into letting her bring up my tray so she could wheedle a juicy story out of me. I decided to sit back and play along.

As I ate, Sister fussed about the room, humming sweetly as she plumped my pillows, opened the curtains, and buttered my toast. It was not until I swallowed my last bite of ham and eggs that she got down to her true business for coming.

After removing the tray, she pulled over a chair and sat down. Taking my hand in hers, she looked deep into my eyes and purred, "Now, Belle, don't you think it's time we had a good long chat? Why don't you tell your big sister what's on your little old mind?" She crossed her heart with a giant X. "I promise not to tell, really I do!"

8

I just had to laugh. "Sister, I hate to disappoint you, but there's just nothing much to tell," I said. "Try as I may, I just can't remember anything about last night."

I sucked in my breath, waiting for an angry reaction. I fully expected her to throw down my hand in disappointment and storm out of the room. But she did nothing of the sort. It then occurred to me: maybe Sister did love me just a little bit.

My heart melted and we began talking like two old chums. As it turned out, she knew more about what happened to me last night than I did. She recounted how my family had spent the evening without me. She, Mother, Father, Mac (my big brother), and Little Henrietta (my baby sister) ate supper at the regular time. Nobody was worried when I didn't show up at dusk. They just naturally assumed I'd stayed overnight at Maggie's because of the rain, as Milindy and I had done just last month.

Things went on quite normally like this until close to bedtime. Sister was upstairs in her room reading when she heard the dogs begin to bark outside. They set up a terrific howl. Someone was in the yard. Grabbing the lamp, she went to the window and looked out.

"The night was pitch black," she said, "and big raindrops were streaking the windowpane. It was almost impossible to see anything outside."

She was just about to give up and return to her book when she spotted something white moving in the woods on the edge of our land. The thing gave Sister a fright; she thought it might be a ghost. She found herself hypnotized by the white phantom. She watched it drift through the trees. Once the white thing left the dark canopy of the woods and entered the open road, Sister let out a big sigh. The "white phantom" was only a small horse. A man was leading it by its reins toward our house. Both made terribly slow progress because they were walking into the driving rain.

As they came closer to our house, Sister saw that the man was leading the horse because something long and lumpy was draped over its saddle, dangling down on both sides, almost to the stirrups. It was hard to see in the rainy dark, but Sister thought it looked like a large rag doll.

As she watched, the man and horse entered our gate, came up the front walk, and disappeared into the breezeway.

Sister wanted to rush downstairs immediately, but remembered she was wearing only a nightdress. By the time she'd found her robe and run downstairs, both man and horse were gone. All that remained was a large puddle in the middle of the breezeway.

"And the lumpy thing across the saddle?" I asked, excitedly. "What happened to it?"

"Oh, that?" she replied, coyly, a wicked smile stealing across her face. "Why, the man gave that to Milindy. Maybe you could ask her."

She knew more than she was telling.

"Sister!" I begged, taking both her hands in mine and shaking them. Only the throbbing in my head kept me from yelling. "Don't keep me guessing! What was it the stranger gave to Milindy?" I braced myself for the answer I knew was coming.

"Belle," she said, looking me squarely in the eye, "it was you."

I swallowed hard. If I came home over the saddle of a stranger's white horse, then where was my own horse? Where was Beauty?

Monday, October 12, 1835

Morning

Ugh! I awoke to the sickest smell. In the night, someone slipped a little red flannel pouch under my pillow. When I opened it, I found the grossest things—rat bones, dried snakeskin, horsehairs, bloody ashes, and other disgusting little bits. It makes me shiver. It's a charm bag—one of Aunty Rachel's magic potions. She thinks something's out to get me.

I threw it under the bed.

Supper

That Milindy! She makes me so mad. I've rung and rung for her, but she hasn't come. I must talk to her! Every time I try to get up to find her, though, the room spins, and I have to lie back down. I must know what happened to Beauty!

Bedtime

Mother came upstairs to tuck me in. She had news.

"Guess what?" she asked, clasping her hands together excitedly. I sat up in bed. "They've found Beauty!"

They'd found her. I closed my eyes and pictured my high-stepping, silky Beauty, how her long, flowing black tail touches the ground when she stands still. Tears stung my eyes. I hadn't lost her after all.

Mother explained. Some hours earlier, a rider had appeared at our door with an urgent letter addressed to "Squire Wood" (my father). The message was from the Baron de La Salle, a wealthy sugar planter from the upper Brazos country.

"This afternoon," wrote the French nobleman,

"your daughter's fine horse was found wandering on my estate. Beauty, I believe the mare is called." The Baron went on to say that Beauty had been munching on some wild parsley haw bushes by the main woodpile when "Moss, my Negro manservant, spotted her. He recognized the beautiful show horse as the famous 'Beauty of Wood's Landing,' and fetched me at once."

Of course Moss recognized Beauty. Moss is family. He grew up here at Wood's Landing. He's Milindy's brother and Aunty Rachel and Uncle Peter's son.

My poor Beauty! We must have become separated coming home, crossing Bailey's Prairie. In a rush, I felt I had to see her. I jumped from the bed and threw on my shawl. But I got up too fast. I saw stars and the room started to spin.

Mother caught me before I hit the floor. "There, there, my pet," she said, helping me back into bed. "Don't worry about Beauty. She's in good hands. The Baron has promised to bring her back to you himself on Friday, when he comes to visit Father. Until then, I must insist that you not leave this bed." She wiped away my tears with her hankie before planting a kiss on my forehead with a firmness that said she considered the matter closed.

Father is holding a big meeting here this Friday. It's

called a "consultation." Men—including the Baron—are coming from all over the colony. Old-timers as well as a few newcomers from the States will attend. It has something to do with our war with the Mexican government. The Mexicans are denying us the freedoms they promised would be ours once we moved from the States to Texas.

Some of the men coming to the consultation want to put together a new Texas government—separate from Mexico's.

Tuesday, October 13, 1835

This morning marked two days without Milindy. According to Toby, who's been bringing my meals, Milindy's been helping Aunty Rachel do chores. Still, you'd think she could have checked on me. I sent word with Toby that I needed to see her. I had to find out what she knew about my mysterious homecoming.

By midmorning, she still hadn't come, and I was out of patience. I threw off the bedclothes, hobbled over to my second-storey window, raised it, and stuck my head outside. "MILINDY!" I yelled toward the backyard, as loudly as I could.

The next voice I heard was not Milindy's but that of

my younger sister, Little Henrietta. She was down below in Mother's rose garden.

"You can't go and bother 'Lindy now, Belle," she said in her soft baby voice. "She's makin' soap!" Little Henrietta was sitting on the ground playing with her black-and-white kitten. She was teasing it by dragging a bit of red yarn through the soft dirt and then yanking it up in the air just as it came within its reach. Each time she played this trick, she giggled. Both she and the kitty were covered in dust.

Little Henrietta stopped her game for a moment and looked up at me. "But if you really, really, really need 'Lindy, you can find her over yonder." She pointed a stubby finger toward the yard behind the kitchen and then returned to her game.

If Milindy won't come to me, by golly, then I'll go to her, I thought. I threw on a dress I found draped over the back of a chair and slipped on some shoes. As I crept down the stairs, I had to grip the handrail. I was shaky, yes, but determined. I had to get to the bottom of this mystery.

I found Milindy out back, stooping over a huge iron kettle, mixing lard, lye, and water to make soap. Just watching her do that made my back ache. Milindy stirred the gooey slop while her mother, Aunty Rachel, kept the fire going underneath. Even little Toby had a job. When big sister, Milindy, gave the signal, Toby reached into a pile of greasy ham bones and tossed a few into the pot.

Those kettles were boiling hot. I don't know how Milindy could stand right over that heat and not melt. I felt close to fainting. I looked to see if Mother was watching. She wasn't, so I wiped the sweat from my brow on my dress sleeve.

Nevertheless, as ill as I felt, I stuck around, pumping Milindy with questions. She apologized for not coming around; she'd just been so busy, she said. She talked as she stirred the pot. Yes, she said, she remembered last Saturday night well. A stranger did indeed bring me home on his pony, as Sister had witnessed.

"Did you catch his name?" I asked, eagerly.

"He didn't give it."

"'He didn't give it'?" I echoed in disbelief. "Well, at least can you tell me what he looked like?" I knew I was being rude but I couldn't seem to stop myself.

"Can't rightly say," she replied slowly, stirring the pot even more slowly, unnerving me with her calm. "He was wearin' a black cloak hidin' his face."

I wanted more than scraps of information. "Whoa!" I said, "Go back and start at the very beginning."

She nodded and began. "It was stormin' something terrible that night. Them dogs was a'howlin' loud! I couldn't get no sleep if my life depended upon it. I got up to see what all the fuss was about. I lit my lantern, threw on my cloak, and headed for the Big House. It was pourin' down rain. By the time I reached the breezeway, I was soaked through and through. When I got there, my heart skipped a beat. There stood a man. He was all dressed in black, but his mustang was as white as milk. And this man—he was a'carryin' a body!"

"Then I saw it was *you* he was a'carryin', Miss Belle! I cried out, 'Lord, have mercy!' and hurried the man inside. With you in his arms, he followed me up the stairs to your bedroom and laid you before the fire."

I looked at Milindy in astonishment. "A man in my room?"

"It all happened so fast and you were drenched to the bone! I turned my back to stoke the fire, and, when I turned back around to speak to him, he was gone!"

"Didn't he say something—anything? Where he'd found me? What had happened?"

"Why, no, come to think of it, he never did say nothin'. Now, wait a minute—I take that back—he did say somethin' to his horse—before he came inside—but that's all. He told it to 'Kay-duh-tay.'"

Because the command to the horse sounded like Spanish, Milindy is convinced that this dark stranger is a Mexican spy. If he is, he's not very clever. What could be more conspicuous than riding a white horse on a black night?

No, this stranger is no spy for the enemy. He's a good fellow. He's my white knight. He must have a good reason for leaving without seeing me awaken or speaking to my parents about what happened. But will I ever find out? Will I ever find him?

Wednesday, October 14, 1835

I'm perking up a bit. My headache is down to a dull throb today. Mother says I'm on the mend and might be able to come out of my room as early as tomorrow.

Mother has a mischievous twinkle in her eye. All afternoon, she and Aunty Rachel have been keeping me company in my room, digging through my clothes trunk, looking for something fetching for me to wear day after tomorrow, when Father's guests arrive for the Friday meeting.

They settled on my brand-new, green and white striped cotton dress. I think it's way too revealing— especially for daytime. Why, the puffed sleeves leave my shoulders completely bare! No matter what they say, I'm wearing my woolen shawl over it.

Sister has been standing in front of the looking glass all day, primping. I don't know how she'll sleep tonight, she's so worked up about all the men coming to our house. She hopes to find a husband among them, I imagine.

Lately, it's been slim pickings for husbands around here. Last month, Col. Stephen Austin sent out the call-to-arms. "There must be no halfway measures! War in full!" he wrote to us in leaflet after leaflet, urging war with Mexico.

This news eventually shut down our school. The boys couldn't concentrate on their studies. They could talk of nothing but war. They have it in their heads that two or three hundred Texians can whip the entire Mexican army. But they can't run off and join the army until they gather the cotton. So last week, Col. Smith closed our country school and sent the boys home to do just that—bring in the crop.

My brother, Mac, will join the Army of the People, too, but only after he and Uncle Peter bring in Mrs. O'Hara's cotton crop. Mrs. O'Hara is Maggie's mother. A few months back, her husband left her. Once Mac has done his part of the harvest, he'll take up the line of march for San Antonio to fight the Mexicans. The president of Mexico is sending more Mexican troops to strengthen the fort there. Col. Austin wants to capture San Antonio.

I imagine most of the guests coming here Friday will be family men from our settlement. However, I did hear Father say that some of the newcomers who arrived in Brazoria from the States last week are coming. For Sister's sake, I hope there'll be a bachelor among them.

Little Henrietta named her black kitten with white spots "Domino."

Friday, October 16, 1835

It's amazing. I've finally remembered what happened last Saturday. Mother has always said that our sense of smell is closely linked to memory. She is so right. Just one whiff of Beauty today, and I was transported back in time six whole days.

True to his word, the Baron arrived here today with Beauty in tow. I was rocking on the front porch when my pride and joy came prancing down the river road. Although I'm still feeling a little puny, I threw down my knitting, gathered up my new skirts, and took off running down our front lane.

I didn't have to look back to imagine what Mother was doing at that moment. I could just picture her, watching from the parlor window, clutching her hankie to her lips "at such unladylike behavior—and, worse, too, in front of the Baron, of all people."

I guess I could have behaved better. I suppose I could have strolled up to his Lordship's fancy carriage, curtsied low and daintily, and offered up my hand for a royal kiss. But all I could think about was Beauty.

I was breathless and dripping with perspiration when I met up with Beauty at the gate. Tearfully, I flung my arms around her neck and buried my nose in her thick mane. She nuzzled me with her own wet nose. In hungry gulps, I drank in her smell—an earthy brew of mud and hay and warm grass that only a horse owner could love.

Her familiar smell jolted something loose in my brain. Suddenly, missing bits & pieces of last Saturday came tumbling into place—

It was long before dawn. Uncle Peter had rung the bell in the quarters. I jumped out of bed and dressed in the dark. Beauty and I needed an early start. We were making a long trip—fifteen miles out and fifteen miles back. We were riding out to Maggie's little log cabin west of Austin Bayou.

Beauty and I were already splashing through the low water ford of the Brazos when the sun had just started to peek over the edge of the prairie. I remember thinking, "I can't wait to see Maggie!" Actually, I was officially going to see Maggie's mother, Mrs. O'Hara, for a fitting. Mrs. O'Hara is making some silk dresses for me to wear when gentlemen come to call. Grandma MacKenzie says that at fourteen, I'm too young to be courted. But she grew up back East. Mother explained to her how things are different here in Texas. With men so outnumbering women, scores of bachelors are desperate for wives.

I don't give a hoot about getting married, but I do like pretty dresses. Why do I have to wait to wear them, though? Anyway, it's a great way to get out to see Maggie.

Oh, how I wish Maggie could go to school with me. Then I could see her more. But Maggie can't go to school. Her mother needs her in the fields and to tend to her baby brother. Their life is such a struggle, especially since Mr. O'Hara ran off with their savings, abandoning them in the wilderness.

Anyway, I spent the morning at the O'Haras' being fitted. I was glad when, around noon, Mrs. O'Hara stopped sticking me with pins and I could get down off that narrow wooden stool. Maggie and I escaped outside, into the cool Gulf breeze.

Somehow the afternoon just slipped away from us. By the time Beauty and I struck out for home and I waved goodbye to Maggie, the sun was dipping low in the sky. I knew I'd be pushing it to cross the prairie, ford the Brazos, and get back to Wood's Landing before dark.

The first half of my trip was easy. Beauty fairly flew across the open and level prairie. We sped by deer grazing under spreading oaks and heard the tinkling bells of grazing oxen. Once we reached the swampy bottomland around Oyster Creek, however, Beauty had to slow to a trot. Stretching up ahead of us was a thick belt of timber bordering the creek. We had reached the canebrake.

The canebrake is a giant bamboo thicket. A road cuts through it. In there, bamboo canes grow twenty feet tall. The canes are so skinny at the top that they flop over the narrow road, forming an archway over us that shuts out the sky. I feel like an ant trapped in a grassy jungle when I ride through the canebrake.

I found the narrow opening that led into the overlapping cane. I didn't like the idea of entering that dark leafy tunnel, yet what could I do? Spooky as it was, it was also the only way home. I plucked up my courage, found where the cane parted to make a road, and urged Beauty in.

Deeper and deeper the road led me inside the cane forest, where both air and light had been sucked away. Snaky vines dangled down from above, slapping me in the face, as I groped my way through on horseback.

I tried to keep my mind on cheerful thoughts, but how could I, with a thousand pairs of hidden animal eyes secretly fixed upon me? Weird little faces kept popping out of holes, blinking, staring, and, then, in an instant, disappearing.

The wild beast smells of the canebrake drove Beauty crazy. Her ears twitched back and forth, and she snorted like an angry bull. To keep her calm, I whispered sweetly in her ear. I knew if she smelled a bear, she'd get scared, dig in her heels, and refuse to go another step. I just had to get her out of there.

By the time we finally crossed the creek, I was a bundle of nerves. My back ached from tension. Every time I had heard a twig snap, I expected a panther to spring on my neck. So you can imagine my relief when at last we burst free from our bamboo dungeon and bounded onto the wide-open spaces of Bailey's Prairie. Misty night was closing in fast, but I wasn't worried. I was on the home stretch. I felt safer.

Until I saw the strange light.

We were galloping into the pecan grove that leads up to the old abandoned Bailey dwelling house when I first saw it. It was far away—at least a quarter of a mile up ahead. It was a white light. It swayed from side to side as if it might be coming from a lantern someone was carrying.

"Oh, goody!" I thought, "Here comes someone to guide me through the dark wood!" But—then—as suddenly as it had appeared—that faraway light vanished.

Now here's the unbelievable part: not ten seconds later, that light reappeared—just six feet in front of me!

The light caught Beauty by surprise and spooked her. She reared up high in the air and whinnied like crazy. The last thing I remember is hitting my head on something very hard. The rest is darkness.

Sunday, November 1, 1835

Yesterday morning, we girls were out in the backyard when Mac galloped up. Milindy, Toby, Little Henrietta, Sister, and I were up to our elbows in pumpkin goo. We were carving jack-o'-lanterns for All Hallows' Eve (which was last night).

"What?" asked Mac, dismounting his horse and walking toward us. "You're not ready yet? Didn't you hear the whistle?" Nobody even looked up at him. We had knives in our hands and had to watch what we were doing.

"Ready for what? What whistle?" I asked, my mind elsewhere. I was concentrating deeply on giving my pumpkin a crooked grin.

"Why, the steamboat whistle, you silly. We've got to get going if we're going to make it before it lands. The New Orleans Greys are coming to Brazoria."

A steamboat! That got our attention. We never miss a steamboat, especially one carrying troops from the States. We threw our knives into the dirt and ran to get Mother. Aunty Rachel went to the rose garden to clip flowers for the soldiers while Uncle Peter hitched up the wagon. Before you could say "Jack Sprat," we were bouncing along on the shady river road, covering the ten miles between our place and Brazoria at a fast clip. It would have been a perfect moment had Father only been there. He, the Baron, and several other of the colonists have gone to San Felipe to continue their "consultation."

Upon reaching Brazoria, we discovered the steamship *Laura* had been expected. Cotton bales and cordwood were stacked on the landing, ready for pick-up. With so many men away at war or consultation, it was mostly women, children, old men, and servants waiting at the dock.

The *Laura* put on a grand show when she finally rounded the bend and chugged into sight. Up the green Brazos River she sailed proudly, parting the glassy water with her wooden prow, flags flying, black smoke billowing from her tall stacks. The crowd cheered wildly. Milindy and I tossed our bonnets into the air.

Sister swooned to see so many good-looking men in uniform. Although they're volunteers, they look like real U.S. soldiers, with their grey matching pants and shirts and sealskin caps. They were packed like mules with equipment—canteens, bedrolls, knapsacks—and lots of weapons—rifles, pistols, swords, and large knives. They looked so grand, they put our ragtag, moccasin-wearing, buckskin-clad Texas volunteer army in the shade.

The sixty-eight Greys have come all the way from Louisiana to answer Col. Austin's call-to-arms. With the promise of free land, they've come to help us separate from Mexico. We tossed roses at their feet as they marched up the gangplank.

Later, on the wagon ride home, Milindy and I chat-tered about the All Hallows' Eve fun we were going to have that night. We talked about how we were going to finish our jack-o'-lanterns. She was going to give her pumpkin crinkly, happy eyes, but I was giving mine slanted, wicked ones.

All that talk about lanterns made me think about the one I think I saw on Bailey's Prairie that Saturday night. Had that strange light come from an ordinary lantern?

I wondered if it had been my white knight carrying a lantern. I asked Milindy, but she couldn't recall whether or not the dark stranger had been carrying a lantern when he brought me home slumped over his white mustang.

Tuesday, November 3, 1835

When I arrived at Mrs. Long's Tavern Sunday night, I entered with a happy heart and smiling face. What a splendid idea to salute the New Orleans Greys with a ball. I was wearing my good purple chintz dress and Milindy had done up my hair in sausage curls.

The dance hall was crammed with soldiers in uniform. Happy couples shuffled to the tunes of Old Joe's fiddle. With the men away at war, I hadn't danced with a boy in ages. My heart pounded with excitement. I was going to have some fun. What if I met someone new? I wondered.

I was at the punch bowl when I spied a young man waving at me wildly above the crowd. Oh, bother! I thought. It was Angus McCoy. "Mercy me, why did he have to show up?" I thought. I had forgotten that Angus might be there. Of course. I should have known. He couldn't go off to war with the other fellows. Once, long ago, he broke his right arm, but it didn't mend properly. He's a terrible shot with a rifle because of it. He lives as a bachelor in a lonely log cabin on a farm way out on Caney Creek.

All night long, Angus trailed me like a puppy. If he wasn't bringing me fruitcake and punch, he was begging for a dance or cutting in on one of my dance partners. Eventually, the other boys gave up. They just assumed I was Angus's sweetheart.

Well, I am no one's sweetheart! Angus wants a wife, and I don't want to get married—especially to a farmer who lives in the middle of nowhere. How odd to even think of striking off and leaving everyone and everything I love behind.

Wednesday, November 4, 1835

The New Orleans Greys left for San Antonio to fight the Mexicans and Mac went off with them. Aunty Rachel made Mac two striped hickory shirts and a knapsack for his provisions. I cut a lock of his hair to place in my Bible. We watched him ride off. Aunty Rachel fought back tears by puffing furiously on her corncob pipe, but Mother, Sister, Little Henrietta, and I cried openly.

San Antonio lies west, outside the country where most families from the States have settled, but it is still part of Texas. It's an important trading post and there's a fort there called the Alamo. On his way there, Mac will cross several rivers. From the Colorado River west is frontier. It's pure wilderness, virtually uninhabited except for hostile Indians. Except for the tiny town of Gonzales, Mac will pass only a few scattered cabins on his way to San Antonio. No one pretends it won't be a dangerous trip.

I wish I'd been nicer to Mac Saturday when he rode up with his exciting news about the steamer's arrival. I was all wrapped up in my silly jack-o'-lantern carving. And now it's too late to make it up to him because he is gone. My big brother has gone to war.

Monday, November 9, 1835

It's so strange to pass the small farms in the surrounding countryside and see mostly women and children picking cotton in the fields. Almost every free man and boy in the settlement with a gun and a horse has left and joined the army. Of course, Uncle Peter is still here as are most of the Negro men who live and work on neighboring plantations.

Everyone around here is picking cotton and talking war. You wouldn't guess the holidays were just around the corner, with the colony so full of working and worrying about war.

A cold snap's coming. Uncle Peter's rounding up the hogs from the woods. He'll start fattening them up with corn, now that winter's on the way.

Father writes that he plans to stay at San Felipe another week. With both him and Mac away, and war looming, Mother is troubled. Her knitting needles click faster and faster as she rocks before the fire.

I don't want her to worry. She's expecting in the spring. If she worries too much, she could lose this babe, too. She can't lose another child; she just can't! Especially after losing my baby brother and sister both to cholera that awful summer of '32.

I was eleven that summer. We buried the two of them up in the peach ridge on the bluff, overlooking the lower field. Uncle Peter made one cross for Amanda Jane and another for Little Willie. We laid flat stones on the graves to keep the wolves away.

Often I visit our family cemetery. With tree branches, I sweep those stones clean. Then I rinse them with water.

Tuesday, November 10, 1835

I've made up my mind. Grandma MacKenzie has stayed with Aunt Polly in Brazoria long enough. It's our turn to have her. I'll write her today and ask her to come and stay with us a spell. Maybe she can help me with Mother during this difficult time—a baby coming, Mac away at war, and Father miles away at San Felipe.

Sunday, November 14, 1835

Toot! Toot! Another steamboat's here—and at our landing, this time! The United States has sent the *Yellow Stone* to rescue our Texas cotton and take it to market! The Mexicans have blockaded the Gulf with a warship and won't let Texas ships pass to take the cotton to New Orleans to sell.

Capt. Ross of the *Yellow Stone* says there's a lot of excitement in the U.S. about Texas. He says that he heard that Mexico is not going to send a large army to Texas. We have heard so many different reports, we don't know what to believe.

I wish we had news from our army! What is happening in San Antonio?

Monday, November 16, 1835

Sister is smitten with Capt. Ross of the *Yellow Stone*. After she went to bed last night, Uncle Peter slept across the threshold of her bedroom door. With Father and Mac away, he's watching over us women and girls like a hawk.

Tuesday, November 17, 1835

It's cold and miserable outside, but still no rain.

Mother, Sister, and I are in Brazoria—but not to pick up Grandma MacKenzie. We visited her this morning at Aunt Polly's. We call Grandma GM. Although she has agreed to live with us for a spell and help us prepare for the baby, she won't be ready to come for another two or three weeks. We'll return to fetch her then.

Meanwhile, we're staying at Mrs. Smith's place with a lot of other women. For two whole days and nights, we've all been melting down lead into bullets.

Everyone is rallying to the cause of building an arsenal for our army. To make bullets, one old neighbor donated the weights of his grandfather clock. Another sacrificed the lead pipes of his aqueduct.

I volunteered to deliver the ammunition. On Friday, I'll take the bag of bullets to a secret location for pick-up by an army scout. My mission is such a closely guarded secret that I won't even be told the drop-off location until some time Thursday. We aren't taking any chances that someone will intercept this priceless load of ammunition for the Texas army. These days, anyone could be a Mexican spy.

Take Father Alpuche, for example. Who would have suspected a Catholic priest of spying for the Mexicans? For years, he moved among us, pretending to be a friend to Texians—baptizing our children, blessing our sick, marrying our young people, and burying our dead. We trusted him and welcomed him into our confidence. But he was no friend. He was just listening to what we said (in English) and then repeating it to the Mexicans (in Spanish). Now we're at war and he's nowhere to be found. What a lowdown scamp! A few of us would like to get our hands on him—

Thursday, November 19, 1835

We received a letter from Father today. The Consultation voted to move the seat of municipal government from Columbia to Brazoria—again. This is the second time they've switched it between the two rival towns. And why? Everybody knows that our town, Columbia, is better suited for visitors going to court. It sits on dry ground on the edge of a large prairie, easy to reach by horse or oxen. Brazoria, however, sits so low in the river bottom that, every time it rains, the roads turn to muck. Nobody can get in or out of town.

The delegates at the Consultation had a hard time agreeing on everything—Texians being so headstrong—but they did elect a temporary government. Henry Smith, my old schoolmaster, was elected governor. Col. Austin's power has weakened. Samuel Houston is our new "major-general," and Edward Burleson has assumed command of our forces surrounding San Antonio.

When the Consultation was over, many of the delegates, Father included, went to join the army camped outside San Antonio. So he won't be coming home—

Father had news of the army. It is tightening the net around San Antonio, which is still occupied by the Mex-

icans. When will our army strike? I pray for God's blessing on Mac and Father and all the men from Columbia
and Brazoria and New Orleans staking their lives so
Texas can be free.

Later

My instructions have arrived. I am to deposit the
bullets "in the hollow of a bee tree twenty paces to the
north of the Old Bailey dwelling house."

That means I have to return to Bailey's Prairie—
alone.

Friday, November 20, 1835

We've all heard the stories, of course, about Bailey's
Prairie being haunted. But, personally, I had never
believed them—until today. It seemed impossible to me
that a grassy meadow so full of birdsong and deer could
be home to a ghost.

And yet today in broad daylight, the old Bailey
house looked positively eerie. Beauty sensed something
creepy about it, too. She hung back, refusing to go
within a hundred yards of the abandoned red cottage. I
was forced to dismount, tie her up, and cover the dis-

tance on foot. I pulled the heavy bag of bullets from behind the saddle and dragged it as fast as I could.

Waist-high weeds choked the path to the front door, scratching my hands until they bled. A mist encircled the red house, giving it a wild and gloomy appearance. I heaved the bag along. I wanted to spend as little time there as possible.

As I rounded the side of the house, I heard the buzzing of a thousand bees. There, just feet away, stood a once great live oak. Bees were swarming in and out of the hollow of its huge, knotty trunk.

I was ready to make my drop when the strangest thing happened. As I was stepping toward the bee tree, I passed through a cold spot. A pocket of icy air seemed to freeze the very ground beneath me. Even though I was wearing my woolen shawl, the unexpected chill gave me goose bumps. I shivered.

I had not yet recovered from that first shock when I got another. My boot heel caught on something jutting up from the path, causing me to trip. I let go of the bag hoping my freed hands could break my fall. Nevertheless, I fell flat on my face. Gritty dirt caked my lips and stung my palms. I pushed up on my sore hands to find I was lying on a stone. Its carving read:

HERE STANDS
JAMES BRITTON BAILEY
1779–1833

It was a tombstone. I was lying on Old Man Bailey's grave.

I was too frightened to move. Then I heard hoof-beats coming out of the woods in my direction.

The rest is a blur. Somehow, I picked myself up, shoved the bag of bullets in the hollow of the bee tree, and ran like lightning toward Beauty. I leaped on her back and rode like the wind, never once looking back. Once home, I flew up the stairs to my bedroom and latched the door behind me. I untied my bonnet and threw it on the bed. Panting for breath, I got down on my hands and knees and felt around under my bed. It seemed like eternity until I found it—the red flannel charm bag Aunty Rachel made to protect me from evil spirits.

I clutched the bag to my chest and, still on my knees, thanked God I was alive. I don't know how long I stayed in that position, clutching the bag, praying. I was finally jolted from my trance by a loud rapping at the door. Of course! In my panic, I'd forgotten. Aunty Rachel and Mother had anxiously awaited my return.

I jumped to my feet and tried to compose myself,

remembering to hide my scratched and reddened palms behind my back (while still clutching the red bag).

"Belle!" cried Mother, rushing to my side. "Is everything all right?" I must have looked a sight. She produced a hankie and nervously dabbed at the perspiration covering my face and neck.

I was surprised to find I still had a voice. "Oh, yes, Mother," I managed to stutter, "yes—everything's fine—perfectly fine. I'm just out of breath from such a hard ride." I longed to reach up and smooth the stray hairs that had fallen from their pins and make myself more presentable, but I couldn't chance letting them see my badly scratched hands. I'd be forced to tell them everything.

I told them only what they needed to know—that the mission was a success; I'd dropped off the bullets as planned. The rest I'll keep to myself. With a war on and a baby coming, they don't need anything else keeping them awake at night—especially if that something else is a ghost.

Tuesday, November 24, 1835

Everything is at a standstill and everything seems dreary.

The *Yellow Stone* is stuck at Wood's Landing. The

Brazos River is too low for it to steam upriver. Uncle Peter heard that farmers from the upper Brazos have piled their cotton bales all along the riverbank from Columbia to Washington-on-the-Brazos, waiting for the river to rise and the steamer to dock. Others who had hauled bales here to our landing ended up storing them in Father's warehouses in Columbia.

When I was in town yesterday, I spotted Dr. Rose from Stafford's Point. He was driving a cart piled high with all kinds of animal skins—from otters, deer, bears, panthers, wild cats, wolves, and coons. He couldn't wait any longer for the steamboat to come upriver to the Henry Jones Ferry, nearer his farm. He needed to sell the skins to buy medicines for his patients. He would have gone to Harrisburg, but there is no drugstore there. Here at Columbia, he can sell his skins, lay in a good supply of drugs, and get a $100 advance on his cotton crop, which he hopes to send to market in May if the ships can get through.

If farmers can't sell their cotton, they can't buy any flour. Without flour, their families will have no bread for the winter. But the Mexican warship won't let our goods pass through the Gulf to market in New Orleans.

There is no working with these Mexicans. They're not to be trusted. They tricked us into coming to Texas and then, once we got here, changed the laws on us. They forced us to become Roman Catholics, yet built us no churches and forbid us to build any ourselves. They gave us no government, yet forbid us to organize our own. Now they're trying to run us off land we bought fair and square! Our land is all we have. We left everything else back in the States.

If the peaceable Col. Austin couldn't negotiate an agreement with the Mexican government, nobody can. I never thought I'd see the day he'd urge us to show open rebellion to Mexico. War is inevitable—we must break free of this dictatorship.

Sister has not a political bone in her body. All she cares about is that Capt. Ross will be here for a good long time, now that his steamship is stuck. There's talk of a Christmas dance for the crew of the *Yellow Stone*. But there won't be much merrymaking, not with our men away at war.

Wednesday, November 25, 1835

Last week, Mr. Wharton stopped by on his way home from the war front. He has left the army for a few days to check on his crops. We were relieved to hear that Father and Mac are doing fine.

For more than a month, he says, our army has been camped outside San Antonio, waiting for the command to attack. Mr. Wharton says our army doesn't have the right ammunition to attack the town. They're also running low on food—and winter is almost here.

Oh, I do hope Mac and Father have enough to eat—and can come home soon.

Friday, November 27, 1835

We were all surprised to receive an invitation from the Baron to join him for Thanksgiving dinner. We wondered, though, why he was home and not fighting at the front with the other men from the colony. Just the same, we were grateful for something to take our minds off the war.

I agonized over what to wear. After much deliberation, I finally decided on my white satin gown and amethyst necklace. Then on the long wagon ride to the Baron's plantation, I regretted that decision. I fretted that I was overdressed.

When we arrived at the Baron's estate, a French butler opened the door. We were standing at the foot of a carved wooden staircase when the Baron made his grand entrance at the top. He wore a black velvet suit trimmed in gold cord, a white ruffled shirt, and a crimson waistcoat dripping with shiny medals and crisp red ribbons. He glided down the steps, greeted us warmly, and slipped his arm through mine. I was escorted into a dining room lit by an enormous chandelier.

I was no longer worried about being overdressed.

Dinner was the most brilliant affair I have ever seen. We ate rabbit soup, bear meat, roasted Irish potatoes, and fresh lettuce and radishes off plates of silver and gold. We drank from crystal goblets. We were at the table four hours. We had so many courses that the servants must have changed the plates fifteen times.

For dessert, we had cream puffs dusted with powdered sugar and shaped like swans. We were transported to another world, a softer one, but over strong black coffee, the conversation finally turned to war. The Baron was agitated over something he had read in the *Telegraph and Texas Register*.

"What if the little Texas army can't stop General Cós?" he demanded, pounding the table. "What if the Mexican army is allowed to march across Texas? What then? Will the soldiers burn our fields? Capture our towns? Free our slaves? Our way of life will be ruined! How can I run my sugar plantation without my Negroes!" His eyes flashed in anger.

As the plates were cleared for the last time and we left the table, I slipped away to look for Moss to thank him personally for returning Beauty. Although the place had been hopping with house servants all night, I had not caught a glimpse of him. Yet I knew that as the Baron's chief manservant, he worked in the Big House. Although I looked everywhere, Moss was nowhere to be found. Curious.

Sunday, December 6, 1835

Today being the Lord's Day, we took the wagon down to Brazoria for a Methodist camp meeting and to pick up GM. Reverend Stephenson had ridden down from San Felipe. In practicing our own religion and not Roman Catholicism, we were breaking Mexican law.

"Are we doing something bad, Mother?" I asked, as we jostled along the river road.

"No, Belle," she said, patting my hand comfortingly, "there are higher laws than Mexican ones."

By law, she explained, we are indeed Mexicans. But in our hearts and minds, we will always remain Americans. And Americans believe in the freedom to worship as they choose. "Freedom to worship as we choose is our greatest good," she said, as we rode into a clearing milling with people, horses, and wagons. It was a huge gathering despite so many colonists being away at war.

It was crowded under the big tent. Reverend Stephenson's face turned bright red when he belted out his mighty sermon.

Once the shouting and the singing were over, the people spilled out into the bright meadow, blinking at the sun's brilliance. Everyone was talking at once. "Will Colonel Burleson ever order our army to attack San Antonio?" was the question of the day. It was rumored that some of our soldiers had lost hope of ever being ordered into battle. They had deserted the army to go home and check on their crops.

Aunty Rachel and I spread quilts on the tall grass. The noonday heat felt good and toasty on my back. We shared our fried chicken and pickles with the Davises and Tennilles, two new families from Missouri. What a tale they told. After they crossed the Sabine, leaving Louisiana, Indians stole their horses and mules. They were forced to abandon their wagon and carry whatever goods they could in their arms or on their backs. Then they had to walk the rest of the way! Of course their shoes gave out and they had to walk barefoot. It took them six months to get here, living off wild game and sleeping on the ground.

On the way out of town, we stopped by Aunt Polly's to pick up GM. Uncle Peter lifted both GM and her trunk into our wagon. GM smells like talcum powder. When she talks to me, she puts her face up so close that we rub nose-to-nose. It makes me cross-eyed. As we talk, she smiles, looks me up and down, and plays with my hair or strokes my cheek. By the way she looks at me, I can tell how much she loves me. Her hugs are the greatest. To fall into my grandma's arms is like sinking into a pudgy loaf of salt-rising dough.

I've never seen GM wear anything but a black silk dress with a cameo pinned at the lacy neck. She wears black because she's still mourning Grandpa MacKenzie's death, though he's been gone a full seven years now. GM cherishes her cameo. It belonged to her mother and her mother's mother before her.

Monday, December 7, 1835

Morning

Last night was the first time since April I have slept without a mosquito net! A blue norther came through after supper, dropping the temperature to a chilly 39°. It was a delicious change from the beastly heat and bugs of yesterday's picnic. I felt so snug in bed, all cuddled up under my down comforter, fire roaring in the grate, bedside candle flickering, book in hand, until I remembered Father and Mac. I could picture them—camped out in the open, the freezing wind blowing, sleeping on a bare and rocky ground. I lay my book on my chest and closed my eyes in prayer for our soldiers.

Bedtime

Milindy sure can be a puzzle. About an hour ago, she came in, as usual, to brush my hair and turn down my bed covers. I was sitting at my vanity, happily humming and arranging a gorgeous bouquet of pink roses the Baron de La Salle just sent me. On the back of his calling card, he had written, "Mon chéri, my heart longs for the next time we two shall meet." I smiled when I read the sweet words, but quickly tucked the card into my vanity drawer when I heard someone coming up the stairs to my room.

It was Milindy. When she spied the roses, her eyes got as big as saucers. "Well, I do say! Pink roses!" she exclaimed. "I simply ADORE pink roses!" I saw her eyes bouncing around the top of my vanity, searching for a man's calling card. But all she could see were a mirror, a brush, and some dusting powder.

She placed her hands on her hips. "Why, Miss Belle!

You've gone out and gotten yourself a secret admirer."

"A secret admirer!" I replied, pretending to be indignant. "Why, I've done nothing of the sort." I produced the Baron's card from the vanity drawer. "See? Here's his card. There's nothing secret about him. His name is emblazoned in gold, swirling letters for all the world to see." I handed her the card, but kept the message side down, hoping she wouldn't turn it over. (Some things are just too personal to share even with good friends.)

When Milindy's eyes came to rest upon the Baron's name, her mouth fell open. A look of horror passed over her face. Her fingers released the card and it fluttered to the floor.

"Milindy!" I exclaimed, jumping up and grabbing hold of her. I thought she might faint. "What's wrong?"

She gulped. ". . . Nothin'," she stuttered, freeing herself from my grip and backing away. She turned away from me and began fussing with my bed covers. She pretended to be absorbed in her housework, but I knew better. Something was terribly wrong.

We said nothing more about the Baron.

Tuesday, December 8, 1835

Angus McCoy came to court me today. I was in the garden picking herbs for Aunty Rachel's sausage making when I heard the dread hoofbeats. I looked down the road and saw him coming. Panic seized my heart. "Hide!" was all I could think.

I dropped to the ground to hide behind the sage and the thyme. But herbs are such short, see-through plants. I needed better cover. On my elbows and knees, I scooted through the dirt between the rows of plants until I reached the cornstalk mounds where we store our vegetables. Like a badger, I burrowed inside one of the mounds and nestled among the sweet potatoes, onions, and turnips. My heart was pounding so loudly I felt sure that Maggie, a full fifteen miles away, could hear it. I crouched still as a church mouse and waited.

I listened as the front door opened and Aunty Rachel admitted Angus into our parlor. I could just picture him waiting: tapping his toes, bouncing his hat on his knee, and licking his fingers to slick down his hair.

A full hour must have passed. Just when I thought I would suffocate under all those root vegetables, I heard Aunty Rachel give the "all clear" signal. "Belle!" she cried from the front door. "You can come on out now, baby. He's done gone!" What a peach she is. I dusted off the corn shucks and sand and ran up the steps to hug her. For a grown-up, she's mighty understanding about what it's like to be young.

I am only fourteen years old. Why, oh, why couldn't there be more single women in this colony? These bachelors are hounding me to death to give up my childhood and become their old married lady. Why can't Angus chase Sister Maurine instead of me?

Later

Tonight, while I was dressing for bed, my mind whisked back to that day I had delivered the bullets to the bee tree. Why had I grown scared and run off? I should have waited to see who picked up the drop.

I've been thinking that maybe it was my white knight who picked up the drop. Maybe, on that rainy Saturday night he found me on Bailey's Prairie, my white knight was there to pick up another pouch of bullets. That would make him a Texas scout, not a Mexican spy.

I wonder if he was carrying a lantern that Saturday night. Milindy doesn't remember his having one. But if it wasn't him carrying a lantern, then how can I explain that weird light?

And another thing—I was thinking about the writing on that headstone. Why does it say, "Here stands James Britton Bailey"? Shouldn't it say, "Here lies James Britton Bailey"? Aren't dead people buried lying down?

Wednesday, December 9, 1835

Aunty Rachel says that some newlyweds are moving into the old Bailey place. They are John and Ann Thomas. They bought the property dirt cheap, she said. Well, of course they did. I wouldn't pay a silver dollar for the whole place. Who in their right mind would want to live in a haunted house?

Friday, December 11, 1835

Enemies, enemies, everywhere. Now the Indians are attacking the families living along the Gulf coast. They know we can't defend ourselves against them. We have no guns. The men in the army took them to war.

Yesterday, Mother received a letter from Col. Austin's sister, Mrs. James Perry. She lives with her family at Peach Point Plantation, near the Gulf beach. She is terrified that the Indians will kill her family. She's sending her three youngest children to stay with us until safer times. Her children are Guy, Eliza, and Stephen. Her husband and two oldest sons are already away at war. Mrs. Perry can't travel at present, as she is expecting a baby any day now.

Milindy and Aunty Rachel are preparing the Bachelor House for the two boys, whereas Eliza will sleep with Little Henrietta.

As soon as Uncle Peter heard that Indians were on a murderous rampage along the Gulf coast, he hitched up the mules and rode out deep into Austin's Bayou to rescue Maggie, her Mother, and her little brother, Patrick. He brought them home with him. They'll sleep safe with us in the Big House.

What a full house we'll have when the Perrys join us—and so many young folk, too. We make five now with Maggie and Patrick. How much fun we'll have, now that it's growing colder and we must stay indoors so much!

Monday, December 14, 1835

Hip, Hip, Hurrah! A courier just rode in from San Felipe with the greatest news. The Texas army finally attacked San Antonio and has captured it. They forced

Mexican General Cós to surrender his soldiers and his fortress, the Alamo, and to leave Texas. What a brilliant victory! Imagine it—our little volunteer army defeating a military force twice its size. It was the brave New Orleans Greys who finally captured the last remaining stronghold of the Mexicans. By now, the Mexican army should have crossed the border and left Texas for good.

Praise God! We read the list of the dead and couldn't find Father's and Mac's names, nor any of our neighbors'.

There is rejoicing all along the Brazos. We're one big family, coming and going from each other's homes like kinfolk. It feels like the Fourth of July in December.

Now that Texas is completely cleared of Mexican soldiers and the war is over, we can have a very merry Christmas. When Father and Mac get home, we'll decorate the house from top to bottom. We'll festoon the mantle with holly and ivy and hang evergreen wreaths on every door. Milindy will tie red bows above the family portraits. Uncle Peter will go out into the woods and cut down the biggest Christmas tree he can find. We'll hang it with balls of cotton and popcorn, shiny ornaments, and long ropes of colored beads. I want candles lit in every window to shout out our joy.

Maybe Mrs. O'Hara will let her family stay and

spend the holidays here. Even though the Mexican danger is behind us, the Indians are still bothersome. We haven't heard any more from the Perrys. I wonder if they're still planning to come? What if both the Perrys and the O'Haras were to be here for Christmas? Then we'd have a built-in party. We could stay up late, play parlor games, pull taffy, and sip eggnog by the fire.

Saturday, December 19, 1835

What a surprise to awaken to birdsong. Here it is, the dead of winter, yet great numbers of red birds are flocking to our garden.

The Texas army is breaking up. Our men and boys are trickling back home. Everyone is so happy to have their loved ones home, safe and sound. I keep dashing to the window, hoping to see Father and Mac ride up.

A letter arrived for me after lunch. It was from the Baron. He would like to escort me to the Christmas dance. In his letter, he promised that:

". . . Should Miss Wood conclude to ride, Le Baron de La Salle assures her Ladyship that the steed, as well as the carriage, shall be of the first order in appearance and in qualities."

Should I accept? The man is easily twice my age! Why, his black hair is already streaked with gray. However, it does make him look rather distinguished—plus, as Mother puts it, the Baron is a "man of substantial property and position"—

Tuesday, December 22, 1835

"It's a miracle he's alive," Dr. Phelps announced to all of us gathered around Father's bed. He then buttoned up Father's nightshirt. Father and Mac are home. At the battle with General Cós in San Antonio, a Mexican sharpshooter shot Father. The musket ball grazed Father's left shoulder, leaving a nasty hole but—luckily—no broken bones.

Dr. Phelps rode ten miles here from his plantation, Orozimbo, to treat his old friend's injury. Father has known Dr. Phelps for thirteen years. They were among the first three hundred Americans who came to Stephen F. Austin's Colony. Father and Mother trekked here overland from Kentucky in a wagon whereas Dr. Phelps left his Connecticut home to sail to Texas aboard a ship called the *Lively*.

Dr. Phelps rolled up the cloth bandages and turned to Mother. "Now, Mary," he said, fixing her with a stern look, "it's going to be up to you to see that the squire gets plenty of rest."

"Yes, Aeneas," she replied. Satisfied that his patient

was in good hands, he gathered up his instruments, tossed them into his black bag, and departed for home.

Mother will have no trouble carrying out the doctor's orders. Father couldn't get up if he tried. He's terribly weak from loss of blood. If it weren't for Mac, he never would have made it home.

Thursday, December 24, 1835

It's Christmas Eve and still no Perrys. It's great having Maggie here, though. When we go into town, we dress alike and pretend we're twins.

I'm so glad to have Father and Mac home.

Tuesday, December 29, 1835

You could have knocked the Baron over with a feather when he came to pick me up for the Christmas dance. He hadn't expected to find both Maggie and me waiting for him. Well, a young lady needs a chaperone. Mother's in no condition to go, and I certainly wasn't going to take GM! It's nice that Maggie's still staying with me and could go as my companion. The weather's still too bad for her family to return to her home.

Being with the Baron means getting a lot of attention. I thought the Widow Rankin's eyes were going to pop right out of her head when she saw me arrive at the dance hall in his fancy carriage with the family coat-of-arms emblazoned on the doors.

At Mrs. Long's, they had pushed the tables back to make a really big dance floor. The Baron and I were having a great time until this new girl began pestering him. I don't know who she is, but I know she can't be from around here.

Anyway, once this girl spotted the Baron, she only had eyes for him. She kept cutting in on our dances. One time, when we were dancing a Spanish reel together, she tripped me—on purpose, I'm sure. She tore my hem in three places!

If the Baron's never seen her before (which is what he claims), then how does she know his name?

Dancing with the Baron is like gliding across a sheet of glass, but I don't like the tight way he holds my waist. It feels pushy. Mother would never approve of so much freshness. I was glad that Maggie was in the carriage with us the long ride home. He didn't dare slip his arm around my shoulders then.

I saw Angus at the dance. So hard to imagine—he was dancing with Maggie!

When the dance was over, I peeked at the horses tied

up at the hitching post. Alas, there was not a white mustang among them.

Wednesday, January 6, 1836

Another excitement! Three of Mrs. Perry's children are going to board with us this spring. They arrived by boat today, accompanied by their servants and even their own schoolteacher, Mr. Pilgrim. Mr. Perry didn't come with them because Mrs. Perry just had a new girl babe. With the Indians still troublesome on the coast, Mr. Perry didn't feel safe leaving his wife and new baby at home.

Mr. Pilgrim will live here, too, and teach all of us lessons. Father's having a schoolhouse built next to the smithy right here at Wood's Landing! It's going to have a real bell. Do you know what that means? I'll get to sleep later on weekdays since I won't be riding out to Gov. Smith's school on the bayou anymore.

The Perry children are Guy Morrison, Eliza, and Stephen. Only Guy is not really a Perry. His last name is Bryan. His father, who died before Guy was two, was Mrs. Perry's first husband. Guy will turn 15 next Tuesday, and has two older brothers in the Texas army.

Guy wants to be a lawyer, like his uncle, Col. Stephen F. Austin. But Guy has trouble reading his law books because of his bad eyesight, so Mr. Pilgrim has asked that I read them to him. I'll be a sort of tutor. Guy brought countless books with him. They are full of Mexican laws—written in Spanish.

I feel let down. I think this fellow may be a bore.

Because he's a houseguest, Guy presented each of us with a small gift. He gave Mother an orange sapling that will grow into a tree that grows real fruit. He gave Little Henrietta a seashell. When you hold it up to your ear, you can hear the ocean. Sister received an embroidered lace handkerchief from New Orleans. And I? What did I receive? A sticky jar of Texas honey!

Saturday, January 9, 1836

Alas, Maggie's gone home. Her mother was anxious to get her family home even if the Indians still do pose a threat. Mrs. O'Hara wants to prepare the fields for February planting.

Father's more like his old self—he's up and about and feeling chipper. Hallelujah!

All the men and the boys from our settlement who went into the army are back at home and hard at work. They all seem to think there'll be no more trouble with Mexico.

Friday, January 15, 1836

For the last three days, I somehow managed to avoid Angus McCoy. But today I got caught. He was waiting outside our new schoolhouse when the dismissal bell rang at noon.

I was walking out the door, carrying a stack of books, when I heard someone say, "Here!" At that same moment, I felt something being shoved into my hands. I looked down to find myself clutching a sack of peppermints. I looked up to see none other than Angus McCoy looking me full in the face.

Oh, no! I thought. Quickly, I turned on my heel and headed, full steam ahead, for the Big House. Halfway there, I halfway remembered my manners, calling back over my shoulder at him, "Oh, thanks for the candy!" But I kept moving. I had to reach the house before he did.

It was no use. He gained on me and was soon by my side, begging me to spend the day with him. I made every excuse I could think of—I had to go meet a friend, wash my hair, return some letters—but he wouldn't let me off. Before I knew what was happening, he had slipped inside our house and planted himself in our parlor.

All afternoon, I endured his courting. The minutes dragged by as we sat in stiff-backed chairs facing one another. Nary a word passed between us. Every so often, Angus would clear his throat and open his mouth as if about to speak, but nothing came out.

Then, along about teatime, Angus suddenly scooted his chair across the room and parked it next to mine.

"Miss Wood," he began, looking meaningfully into my eyes. "I think I can offer you a nice . . ."

Alarm bells—not wedding bells, as Angus would have had it—went off in my brain. Anybody watching at that moment would have thought I'd sat on a sewing needle! I sprang from my chair, dashed to the front door, and yanked it wide open.

Fortunately, just at that moment, Sister and Guy were coming up the front walk. "Sister! Guy!" I yelled. "Come and join us for a game of cards!" They read my distress and instantly rushed to my aid.

We got a game of whist started. We almost had to quit because Angus doesn't know how to play cards. But Sister and Guy got the drift and we kept playing anyway until finally evening came, and Angus rose to go. I breathed a sigh of relief, fully expecting him to head home. He'd never left his cows this long before. But, to my despair, he informed me that he was not going home but spending yet another night at a hotel in Columbia.

He also told me he's coming back to see me in the morning.

EEEEK!

Saturday, January 16, 1836

This morning I awoke to the sound of pebbles hitting my bedroom window. Was it hailing? I wondered. I stumbled blindly to the window to see. In the grey, predawn light, everything looked fuzzy. But I could see plainly that the weather was clear. It was certainly not hailing.

I was aiming to get back in bed when I spied some movement down below in the rose garden. It was a young man. He was waving his arms wildly at me. I rubbed my eyes. It was Guy Bryan!

In raising the window, I was hit by a blast of cold air. I hugged my gown to me and shivered.

"What on earth are you doing?" I called down to Guy, breathing out frost.

"Good morning!" he called up in a forced whisper. "Get dressed! We're going riding!"

"Riding?" I called back, so loudly that he shushed

me up with a quick finger to his lips. I tried to be quieter. "What? Riding? At this hour? Why, the sun's not even up!"

"Exactly!" he replied. "That means we'll have the whole countryside to ourselves. Hey—don't you like adventure?" Disappointment crept into his voice. "Okay—fine—I just thought I'd ask—I'll be leaving the stables in ten minutes—should you change your mind." Then he was gone.

What was wrong with me? I love adventure.

I knew that if I hurried, I could still make it. I didn't even bother to shut the window. I yanked off my nightclothes and tossed them in a heap. I splashed cold water on my face and ran my fingers through my hair. I threw on my riding outfit, boots, and hat, and grabbed my whip. I was so afraid Guy would gallop off without me that I didn't even glance in the mirror! In just a few minutes, I was down at the stables, ready to ride.

Thank goodness he was still there. He had thought of everything. He'd packed us a picnic lunch and saddled up our two ponies. I rode Beauty, and he rode one of our horses, Chestnut, another of our prized Morgans. Guy's favorite horse, King, is still down at Peach Point, but he hopes to bring him up here sometime soon.

Galloping across the prairie on a raw January morning brought color to my cheeks. We rode toward the coast, where long-legged cranes stalked in the tall grass and we could hear the roar of the ocean.

The hours sped by, as we rode about the country. The salty sea breeze and the exercise gave us big appetites. We devoured the crackers and cheese, laughing and talking like old friends. I can't remember when I've had more fun.

When we arrived home, Milindy was waiting for me at the back door. She handed me a letter. She peered over my shoulder as I read it. It said:

Dear Miss Wood,

I am not a turtle that carries its house on his back. I live thirty miles from here and the watercourses are difficult to cross. If I come to see you often, I shall make no crop. I will be back in one week. I will expect an answer from you then.

Yours truly,
Angus McCoy

I wadded it up and tossed the letter in the fire.

Later, I ran into Guy—who'd heard about the letter.

"There's no denying it, Belle, this Angus fellow has set his cap for you. He's going to settle for nothing

64

short of having you for his wife," he said. "Yes, Angus will make some girl a fine husband some day. He's got a nice herd of cattle and hogs. That land of his is pure peach and cane bottomland, the best there is this side of the Colorado. Yes, a girl could do worse than marry old Angus McCoy." Then he smiled and winked.

I started to get angry, then smiled back. I realized he was teasing. Guy may be puzzling, but he's a lifesaver. For two days in a row, he's kept me from being alone with Angus. Do you know what I'm going to do when I finish writing this? I'm going downstairs and bake Guy the best cherry pie he's ever sunk his teeth into.

Monday, January 18, 1836

I rode into Columbia this morning to meet the mail boat—still no letter from the Baron. I've heard nothing from him since the dance. That was three and a half weeks ago. You'd have thought I'd heard something from him by now—

While I was walking away from the dock, who do you think I saw getting off the boat from Orozimbo? It was that mean girl from the dance, the one who ripped my skirt. A Negro man was helping her and her maid into a wagon and putting their trunks in the back.

I was hiding behind a post, spying on her, when I felt

a tap on my shoulder. I shrieked and jumped. I wheeled around to find the Widow Rankin wagging a plump finger at me.

"Missy," she announced, in a tone loud enough for any passerby to hear. "I like you. You come from a good family." She raised her voice even more. "Why, then, are you keeping company with a scoundrel like the Baron? Has his money turned your pretty head? Missy, I tell you, that man's bad—bad to the bone!"

People had stopped to stare. I could feel my ears turn crimson. I was so stung by the Widow's nasty remarks that I could not speak. Before I could gather my wits about me, though, she had tossed her head, bid me a pert "Good day," spun on her heels, and disappeared into the dry goods store.

This wasn't the last trouble I'd see today. Another rude shock awaited me upon my return home. That awful girl I saw disembarking at the Landing. There she sat with her maid—in my own parlor. Her name is Priscilla Pruitt. She's from Bolivar. Mother says she's going to be our houseguest for a spell. She's going to sleep in my bedroom with me and attend our school!

It was Dr. Phelps who suggested the arrangement to Priscilla's father, a widower who runs a blacksmith shop in Bolivar. Mr. Pruitt then wrote Mother, who, of course, said yes, she'd be delighted to have Priscilla board with us.

Is there no end to Mother's Christian charity? Enemies, enemies, everywhere, and, now, one is installed in my very own bedroom—

Tuesday, January 19, 1836

How I love cozying up next to a warm fire when it's cold and wet out of doors. That's how we ladies passed an agreeable day today—just rocking and sewing and chatting by the fire. Even Priscilla proved to be good company, plunking out tunes on the piano to liven it up.

The fire was so pleasant that, by midafternoon, Little Henrietta and Eliza grew drowsy-eyed. We waited for Milindy to come and put them down for their regular nap. But I rang and rang and she never showed up. I ended up taking the two sleepyheads upstairs myself.

After tucking the girls in, I went to the bedroom window to close the curtains. From Little Henrietta's room, I could see the back buildings of our estate. The rain was pouring down, turning the path from the smokehouse to the servants' quarters into a sea of mud.

A thin ribbon of hickory smoke curled up from the smokehouse chimney. My mouth watered at the smell of sweet bacon curing.

As I was watching, I saw someone exiting the smokehouse door. It was Milindy! She was carrying a big bundle under her shawl. She checked to see if the coast was clear before darting toward her quarters. She ran through the rain like she was running for her life. Each time a foot landed in a puddle, mud splashed up onto her long, white apron.

What on earth is she up to?

Wednesday, January 20, 1836

A brisk and blustering norther blew in today. It's freezing cold. Drat! I had so wanted to put in my winter garden today.

I'd been thinking about that command my white knight gave to his mustang when he rescued me from Bailey's Prairie. "Kay-duh-tay" sounds like Spanish to Milindy, so I decided to ask Guy if he'd ever heard the expression before. He knows Spanish so well.

He didn't skip a beat before answering. "Well, sure, I know what *¡Quédate!* means. That's what you tell your horse when you want it to stay put. Why do you ask?"

"Oh, just curious," I replied, lost in thought. So it is Spanish. But that doesn't mean my white knight has to be a Mexican spy, like Milindy thinks. There could be another reason. He might speak Spanish to his horse because, after all, it is a Spanish mustang—

Thursday, January 21, 1836

The water in my pitcher froze solid last night. What is wrong with Milindy? She let the fire go out in my room.

Friday, January 22, 1836

Morning

The sun rose on a beautiful frozen prairie—it glittered like a sea of glass in the winter sunshine. A silver frost covers the trees. "It's as cold as the Boston Commons," said Mother at breakfast. In her youth, she spent some time in Massachusetts.

Afternoon

The one (and only) thing Priscilla Pruitt has going for her is her name—it fits. She is nothing but a prissy girl.

"Guy, how do you like my dress?" she said today in class, twirling around and around, so that her skirt encircled her like a wreath. What a flirt. From now on, I'm calling her Prissy.

Saturday, January 23, 1836

The day began with cold, driving rain. We had planned to dine tonight at the Varners, but had to cancel because of the weather. Everyone is gloomy—but not I!

How could I be? This is the Saturday Angus vowed to return. But—oh, glee!—the roads have turned to slush and—oh, bliss!—the babbling brooks have become foaming rapids. This chaos in nature makes me wildly happy! Because I know that, under such conditions, Angus McCoy cannot possibly travel to Wood's Landing today.

Sunday, January 24, 1836

With three fields to plant, Father had to hire six of Col. Varner's Negro slaves to help put in the corn crop. They got here yesterday, but did no work today. Sunday is the Lord's day—a day of rest—on our plantation.

Tuesday, January 26, 1836

I never thought I'd see the day I'd be glad Prissy lived under our roof. But there you have it, I'm glad. I'm not just glad, I'm grateful. Grateful to God that tonight, when I turn out the light, she'll be sleeping in the bedroom with me. Because if she weren't here, I'd be alone in the dark. Then I'd never be able to close my eyes. Not after what Aunty Rachel told us tonight.

She says there is a ghost at Bailey's Prairie. The woman who just moved there—Mrs. Thomas—saw it.

It happened a few weeks ago, said Aunty Rachel. Mr. Thomas had gone away for the night leaving Mrs. Thomas alone at the red cottage with her maid.

Both women were sleeping when something caused Mrs. Thomas to wake up. She sat up in bed. As she did, she felt a wave of cold air pass over her body. She wrapped her arms around her chest. Something strange had come into her room.

She strained to see, but it was so dark she could not even see her maid's cot across the room. Then, in the doorway, something moved. It was huge and had the body of a man. But the body was not solid like a man's. It was blurry—shifting—and faceless.

This—thing—floated toward Mrs. Thomas, reaching for her. She tried to scream, but the scream froze in her throat. She couldn't move. It bent over the bed. Just when she thought it was going to grab her, instead, it reached down under her bed. It was searching for something. It was then that Mrs. Thomas found her voice. She let out a big scream. It had to be a ghost because just like that, it vanished into thin air.

When Mr. Thomas returned, his wife told him she had seen a ghost. He scoffed at her, accusing her of having "another one of her nightmares."

If that's the case, then how would Mr. Thomas explain what happened to me when I felt that chill rise up from old Bailey's grave? Would he label my story a "daymare"? Men are so quick to pass off women as hysterical!

What was that ghost looking for under Mrs. Thomas's bed?

Friday, January 29, 1836

There's so much work to be done and still not enough men to do it. Mac, Guy, and Uncle Peter are splitting rails to repair the back string of fence in the bottom field. Even with his tender shoulder, Father's working alongside the field hands to clean up the corn ground.

Next week, we plant the corn.

Monday, February 1, 1836

Here's the latest excitement. A messenger came to our house from Goliad with a dispatch. It said that a Mexican from the Rio Grande arrived at Goliad and informed Col. Fannin that shortly General Santa Anna, the president of Mexico himself, will cross the river into Texas with a large army. This army would then advance in two divisions, one toward Goliad and the other toward the city of San Antonio.

Not everyone believes this report. Gov. Smith, though, believes it plenty. He has ordered Col. Travis, a lawyer from San Felipe, to hasten to the Alamo, the Texas fort most vulnerable to Mexican assault. He has asked Col. Travis to raise a hundred volunteers to take with him. But it's corn planting season. The men can't afford to leave their fields just yet. Anyway, most men around here don't expect any more trouble from Mexico, not since General Cós was so firmly trounced two months ago. They consider placing more troops at the Alamo just a precautionary measure. As a result, only twenty-nine volunteers from around here left their crops to follow Col. Travis to the Alamo. My brother Mac, I'm proud to report, is among those twenty-nine. So Mac's gone again to San Antonio.

Not everyone likes Col. Travis, but I do. On one of his visits to Wood's Landing, he brought Sister and me Sunday school books.

Some folks call him a troublemaker. They blame him for our trouble with Mexico. Santa Anna, the president of Mexico, has issued a warrant for his arrest. Santa Anna's smart to want Col. Travis stopped. "He's a born leader of men and an excellent soldier," says Mac. That's why Texians do what he says and why Mac couldn't resist following him.

Guy wanted to enlist, too, but Father persuaded him to continue being a "home guard" in the Colony. I didn't know Guy was a home guard.

"What does a home guard do?" I asked him.

"Oh, nothing much. . . ." he replied, blandly. His words didn't match his expression, though. Even behind those thick glasses, I could detect a mischievous twinkle in his eye.

Hmmm. . . . So Guy has a secret. . . .

Friday, February 5, 1836

Still planting corn and breaking up land. There's more work now that Mac's gone. We're lucky Guy's here.

I guess I can give up on hearing from the Baron. Although I haven't felt quite the same about him since that encounter with the Widow Rankin, it still hurts my pride not to hear from him. I was under the impression he liked me. What about those roses he sent me?

Prissy came to breakfast today, but skipped our morning classes. Then after lunch, she appeared at school for afternoon classes wearing pearl earbobs I've never seen her wear before. Are they new? If so, then where did she get them?

Tuesday, February 9, 1836

I can barely grip this pen, my hand is trembling so.

The afternoon started off so mildly, too. There I was, quietly writing letters in the parlor when, all of a sudden, I heard the barking of dogs so deafening, my spine tingled. I thought the hounds of hell were descending upon us. I sprang to the window. A huge pack of hunting dogs, yelping, jumping, snapping, and growling, was charging out of the woods, heading straight for our house. One look at their sharp and pointy teeth and I instinctively clutched my throat. Thank the Lord for our fence.

A man with a hat pulled down low over his eyes rode with the pack. Judging by his looks, GM would have called him a no-good scoundrel. The stranger rode up to our gate.

Within seconds, Guy appeared, Kentucky long rifle in hand. (Father's away for the day, so Guy's in charge.) Guy held the gun on the man and wouldn't let him get down off his horse.

I raised the window so I could hear what they were saying, but, with so much barking, I still had to strain to hear. The stranger told Guy he works for the Baron, overseeing his slaves. One of the Baron's slaves has run away, he said. He said the runaway slave is Moss and that bloodhounds had traced his scent to Wood's Landing! The overseer was sure Moss was hiding on our property. He demanded to search it.

Guy was quick. "May I see the Baron's letter authorizing you to conduct such a search?" he asked, coolly, holding out his hand to receive such a letter.

The overseer frowned. "Letter?" he cackled, holding out empty hands. "I ain't got no letter. All I got is my orders—orders from the Baron himself to bring back that runaway slave—dead or alive!"

"No letter—no search!" Guy replied, firmly. He then raised his rifle and leveled it at the overseer's beady eyes. "I'm afraid I must order you to leave—at once." Guy sounded calm, but he cocked his gun. "Or else I will be forced to shoot you for trespassing on private property."

The overseer turned his horse around and raced for the cover of the woods, whimpering hounds loping behind. Before vanishing into the trees, however, the man shook his fist at Guy and shouted back over his shoulder, "You'll be sorry for this, sonny boy!—'cause I'll be back—and I'll get him, too, mark my words, I'll get that blasted troublemaker." GM would have been right. That man was a scoundrel.

When the coast was clear, I ran outside to join Guy. I wanted to squeeze him hard for his courage (and lawyerly skill), but we're not on such terms (yet?). We headed straight for Aunty Rachel and Uncle Peter's cabin where, sure enough, we found Moss, sitting on a cot, his head buried in his hands.

Moss wept as he told of his former life. The overseer, he said, is unspeakably cruel. He delights in whipping the Baron's slaves. Earlier in the fall, Moss had learned that the overseer had whipped a female slave. Moss told the Baron about it, assuming he'd care and put a stop to such evil. The next day, however, Moss was demoted from house servant to field hand (which explains why I didn't see him at Thanksgiving dinner). The Baron avoided Moss from then on.

Then, about three weeks ago, Moss was working in the fields, planting sugar cane, when he heard a frantic cry for help. He dropped his hoe and ran in the direction of the cry. Behind the woodshed, he came upon a terrible scene. The Baron's overseer was whipping a little black boy he had tied to a pole.

Moss saw red. He grabbed the whip out of the overseer's hand, and began whipping him with his own weapon. The overseer fell backwards, hit his head, and was knocked unconscious.

"Run!" shouted Moss's friends, watching from afar. "Run for your life!" So Moss ran, crossed the Brazos, and snuck down to Wood's Landing, where he knew he'd be safe. Had he stayed at the Baron's, there'd be no thirty-nine lashings for this escape. Moss would be a dead man.

Moss sobbed at the memory. When Guy patted him on the back to comfort him, Moss winced in pain. Guy lifted Moss's ragged shirt to reveal a back striped with torture—torture inflicted by a bullwhip on bare flesh. From his shoulders to his waist, Moss's back was marked by old, healed-over, bumped-up scars that criss-crossed with fresher, scabby cuts.

We'll help Moss—that means harboring a fugitive slave—a serious offense.

Poor Moss. How can he ever rest? The yelping of those dogs haunts my dreams. They wanted to tear Moss from limb to limb. That overseer had no intention of delivering Moss to the Baron alive.

To be born a slave—how terrible!

Wednesday, February 10, 1836

We finished corn planting this morning.

Father is back from government business in Brazoria. Guy told him about Moss. Moss is hiding in the corn crib. Milindy and I put black pepper in his socks and sprinkled tons of it all around the plantation grounds. If those bloodhounds come back, they'll be so busy crying and sneezing from the pepper, they'll totally forget about hunting down Moss.

Oh, now I see. That day I saw Milindy running from the smokehouse in the rain? The bundle under her arm must have been a side of bacon she was taking to her starving brother Moss in hiding. Poor Milindy—no wonder she's so distant lately and so private. What a frightening burden to carry.

Prissy is into some kind of mischief. Milindy says Prissy's maid, Flo, told her that Prissy has all kinds of nice, new things besides the pearl earbobs. In class, Mr. Pilgrim scolds Prissy because she won't keep her mind on her lessons. Prissy just shrugs and smiles a secretive smile.

Thursday, February 11, 1836

Last night, I woke up in the middle of the night and Prissy wasn't in her bed. The next time I saw her was at breakfast. She came breezing in—late—with dark circles under her eyes.

"Where have you been?" I whispered to her, over bowls of hot corn mush. She made up some nonsense about not being able to sleep and going for a walk to calm her nerves.

Walking in the freezing night air to relax? I doubt it. I think Prissy snuck out to meet someone—a man. I'm certain of it—a rich man who showers her with outrageously expensive gifts. Because around her neck hung a brand new string of pearls. This new necklace matches her pearl earbobs perfectly.

Oh, no. It's starting to rain. It'll wash away all that pepper and Moss will be discovered!

Friday, February 12, 1836

Noon

This morning, Prissy, Sister, and I were sent to the prairie field to keep the birds from eating the newly planted corn. At first, I dreaded being with Prissy—she can act so saucy. But, to my surprise, she was musical and funny today. The three of us girls made up silly songs to scare away the crows. We whirled around in dancing circles until we got dizzy and fell down, laughing, in the damp dirt. I fear we crushed a few seedlings—

Evening

We didn't have to repepper the yard to protect Moss because, this afternoon, Father and Guy smuggled him aboard a flat boat heading downriver with a load of cotton. Before reaching the Gulf, the boat will dock at Peach Point Landing where Guy's stepfather, Mr. Perry, will pick up Moss and take him to his plantation. For now, Moss will be safe—we hope.

I was all wrong about Guy. When I met him, I thought he'd be lumpish, just because he wears thick glasses. How many men would stick their necks out to protect a slave from a wicked master? Guy is a prince among men.

Saturday, February 13, 1836

It's a good thing we whisked Moss away yesterday because today that mean skunk of an overseer showed up again. And this time, he brought not just his hounds but the Baron himself. Evidently, the Baron has been staying in Columbia for the last few days.

Father met the men at the gate. I watched, hidden, from an upstairs window. I couldn't hear much of what the three men were saying, but I could tell from Father's body movements that he was being very businesslike with the Baron, not warm and congenial as he has always been with him in the past. Although Father did let them search our entire grounds, including the slave quarters, he did not invite the Baron into our home.

Some time later, I watched as the two men rode off with their dogs into the cold woods. I felt sinful delight to see them leave so empty-handed and insulted.

I'm still in shock about the Baron—and ashamed of myself, too. I fancied him my beau. I guess I was so enchanted by his French title, his crystal chandeliers, fancy carriage, and velvet waistcoat that their glitter blinded me to the truth: the Baron has a black heart. How can a man beat the very people whose sweat and toil have made his life so comfortable? The Widow Rankin was right. The Baron is a very bad man.

My skin crawls to remember how, just seven weeks ago at the Christmas dance, his nasty fingers slipped around my waist. What a rotten judge of character I've been. I've been pining away for a wicked beast.

Friday, February 19, 1836

A thousand rumors are afloat.

Mr. Dyer and his wife just stepped off a boat from New Orleans, where they heard lots of talk about Texas. We pressed them to stay overnight before returning to their home at Stafford's Point. We were greedy for the latest news.

A Frenchman told Mr. Dyer that not one, but two Mexican armies were marching toward our border. We've heard that news before. We just don't know whether it's true. No one around here really expects more trouble from Mexico. We're keeping some soldiers at the Alamo just in case.

Also on their voyage across the Gulf, the Dyers didn't spot a Mexican warship blocking the mouth of the Brazos.

"Well, that's a good sign, isn't it?" I asked Father, thinking that if the warship had sailed away, the Mexicans had possibly called off an attack on Texas.

"Not necessarily, Belle," said Guy, jumping into the discussion. "If the Mexicans do come after us again, they won't come at us from the Gulf—too many sandbars and reefs for their ships to get hung up on. Anyway, they wouldn't have a chance of breaking through. Our rebels have firm control of the coast."

Father nodded. "Guy's right, Princess," he said, puffing on his pipe and taking my hand in his. "If Santa Anna does return with his army, he'll come by land—in the spring—at the very earliest. In that way, he'll be sure there's plenty of green grass to feed his horses."

Well, at least our boats are now free to carry our cotton to market in Louisiana again.

Monday, February 22, 1836

Well, Father was dead wrong. Santa Anna is already in Texas. He didn't wait for any spring grass. At the very moment I write these words, the Mexican dictator's army is marching toward San Antonio—and the Alamo. This time, it was our spies who spotted his soldiers crossing the Rio Grande, so we trust our information. Santa Anna is charging here in the dead of winter, fueled by anger, they say. He's furious at the way General Cós was driven out of the Alamo, San Antonio, and then Texas by our little volunteer army last December. It is rumored that General Cós is Santa Anna's brother-in-law.

Some say Santa Anna is coming to run us all east to the Sabine River and back into the U.S. Others say Santa Anna won't leave until he kills every American Texian.

Guy is itching to go to war. His older brothers, Joel and Austin, have already joined the Texas forces.

"I'm no coward," protested Guy, as he split logs for our woodpile. "I would fight Santa Anna at every creek, river, and thicket all the way from the Rio Grande to the Sabine." But he can't leave Wood's Landing to fight. He's already been assigned an important duty, guarding the home front. We depend upon his protection—and Father demands it. I just wish Guy thought being a home guard was as important as fighting in the army. I think he'd like to trade places with Mac and maybe become a war hero.

Tuesday, February 23, 1836

An icy wind blew in today, and with it, a storm of rain.

We greeted the *Yellow Stone* once again. It stopped by on its trip upriver, to pick up more cotton to send to New Orleans. With the river on the rise, Capt. Ross can chug his steamboat clear up past San Felipe, maybe even up all the way north to Washington-on-the-Brazos. That's where Father will be next week, at the convention. He'll be a delegate from Columbia. Now more than ever, Texas must separate from Mexico. This convention will create a new body of laws and elect a permanent government.

Sister was beside herself to see Capt. Ross again. Uncle Peter was worried to death that she would stow away on the *Yellow Stone* before it shoved off. But she didn't. Nevertheless, where romance is concerned, one should never underestimate Sister.

Thursday, February 25, 1836

Noon

What can it mean? A long line of men, women, and children are passing by our land on their way to Columbia. They are traveling in every kind of vehicle imaginable—wagons and truck carts, sleds and sleighs. Some ride horses or mules. I saw one man riding a cow. Although the weather is wet and cold, many of the women walk barefoot, with no covering for their heads. Some carry children atop their shoulders. They look hungry, tired, muddy, and ragged.

What was this odd parade? We had to find out. All of us here at Wood's Landing, whether studying in school, toiling in the fields, or cooking in the kitchen, dropped what we were doing and ran down to where our front lane meets the Columbia road.

Once there, we shouted, jumped up and down, and waved at the passersby, but no one paid us the least bit of attention. There was so much noise and confusion. Babies were crying, wagons groaning, wheels creaking, hoofbeats pounding the muddy, pitted earth, and teamsters shouting at oxen. No one answered our calls. Everybody kept right on moving toward town. They were all going somewhere in a great big hurry.

Finally it was Father who got the story. He approached a black man straggling by on foot, tending a pair of slow-moving oxen pulling his master's wagon.

"We're refugees," said the black man, nodding to the people in the wagon behind him. Father walked alongside as the man told his story. "Do you know where San Patricio is—way south near the coast? We live near there. A few weeks ago, some men on horseback came riding through our settlement shouting, 'Run! Run! Run for your lives! The Mexicans and Indians are coming up the coast, burning and killing everything in their path!'"

The alarm threw many people into a blind panic, he said. Many fled their homes instantly, leaving doors wide open, beds unmade, half-eaten meals left on the tables, and chickens and cows running loose in the yard. "Those people just plain lost their heads." he said. "They left without packing what they needed to survive."

"But not us," he boasted, pointing proudly to the wagon. "We kept our wits about us and took everything we could." They had indeed. The wagon was stacked to the teetering brim with mountains and mountains of stuff. (No wonder the oxen were so slow—they were worn out!) I spied a rocking chair, a chest of drawers, cooking pots, bundles of clothing, mattresses, sacks, crates, and barrels of food. Grannies, brothers, aunts, babies, and assorted other kinfolk—both black and white—peered out at me from within the wagon. They were squeezed in among the clutter.

With their cattle, horses, and Negroes, all of these moving people are running from the Mexicans and heading to safety—at the U.S. border.

Later

The winding line of runaways continues to drift by our door. The line continues backward and forward as far as the eye can see.

Angus McCoy sent word that a group of refugees from Refugio is hiding near his farm. They're taking cover in the canebrake along Caney Creek. They're not running east. They believe that Fannin's troops at Goliad can beat back any Mexican forces that might come up the coast. Once a Texian victory is achieved, they plan to return to their homes.

Guy rode off without a word this afternoon and has yet to return.

I must wake up early tomorrow if I am to see Father off. He's leaving early for that convention at Washington-on-the-Brazos.

I hear the Baron's in Columbia. He won't be darkening our doorway any time soon.

Friday, February 26, 1836

What was once a trickle of moving people is now a steady stream. It's making people around here panicky. They think of fleeing, too.

As justice of the peace, Father needed to calm the public's fears. He had to postpone his travel plans and call for an emergency community meeting. Messengers rode out to the distant reaches of the colony to spread the word.

By midafternoon, a mob of chattering, nervous people had gathered at our house. Father cleared his throat for silence before addressing the group.

"Neighbors, friends!" he cried, his voice filling with strong emotion. "Are your memories short? Have you already forgotten how—less than three months ago—your fellow Texians routed the last Mexican army to cross the Rio Grande? Have you lost faith in your own army? The Texian forces under Col. Fannin at Goliad and Col. Travis at the Alamo are MIGHTY MEN! I guarantee you that with every ounce of their strength, they'll prevent the enemy from crossing the Colorado River and occupying our settlement." He beseeched the crowd to stay on their land and not to run.

As the people filed out of our house, it was hard to tell by their faces whether Father's speech had made any difference. Would they stay or run? I don't know about the others, but I can tell you this much: we're not running! We have work to do. We have deep roots in this land! With the corn up and growing, there's hoeing and plowing to be done, to keep out the weeds. Then we have to put in the sweet potatoes, beans, cabbage, and peas. If we don't plant and hoe now, come summer, what will we eat?

Anyway, Mother's in no shape to travel, with the baby coming in April—and GM is much too old to bump along in a rickety wagon across an uncharted countryside.

When Father finally did manage to leave for the convention, there was just enough daylight left for him to make it to Capt. McNeel's place by nightfall. After an overnight stay there, he'll have to ride like the devil to reach Washington by Tuesday. I wept to see his horse disappear down the road.

Wait a minute—here I am ready to put my diary away and to blow out the candle for the night, yet Prissy's not in her bed. Where could she be? Now that I think of it, I don't recall seeing her at the afternoon meeting. Matter of fact, I haven't seen her all day!

Surely she didn't join the throng of fleeing people, did she?

Saturday, February 27, 1836

Now for more news of the unexpected: Col. Fannin and his 500 men plan to abandon the fort at Goliad and proceed at once to the Alamo.

Many of our neighbors are relieved to hear this. With Fannin reinforcing Travis, that gives the farmers a bit more time planting their crops before they, too, have to leave for the Alamo.

Other neighbors received the news quite differently. They are terror-stricken. With no soldiers at Goliad, they argue, a Mexican army could march straight up the coast and invade our colony unopposed. You'd think the Mexican army was right on our doorstep, to hear these frightened people carry on.

Some people are already hiding their valuables in the river bottom.

Sunday, February 28, 1836

After being gone on a mysterious mission for four days, Guy is back—with juicy news.

We were having our Sunday dinner when he pulled up a chair.

Aunty Rachel handed him a plate. "Remember those

men who rode through San Patricio and the other southern settlements, shouting, 'The Mexicans are coming!'?" Guy asked, helping himself to platters of pork roast, potatoes, biscuits, and gravy.

"Yes?" we answered at once, hungry for news.

"Well, they weren't Texian scouts," he explained, "and no Mexicans were coming. Those men were criminals—spreading a false alarm around the countryside so the people would evacuate their homes. Then, after everyone had fled, the imposters went in and looted all their valuables. I saw the ransacked buildings myself." He polished off the last of his food and reached for second helpings.

In between more bites, he went on to say that while in San Patricio, he had met with Col. Frank Johnson, the commander of a small detachment of Texian troops stationed there. Col. Johnson's scouts have not sighted any Mexican armies in the area.

We breathed a sigh of relief to hear such encouraging news. Also, it was just plain good to have Guy back under our roof again.

So now I know what being a "home guard" means! It means spy. Guy's a spy. Hey, that rhymes.

We still have not seen Prissy since Thursday. So after dinner, alone in my bedroom, I latched the door behind me and lifted the lid of Prissy's cedar chest. It was half empty. Prissy had taken her best dresses and left behind her everyday calicos and bonnets.

Now I could understand her packing silks and satins for a pleasure trip. But not for traveling with the movers heading east, who are bound to cross rising rivers and muddy prairies—

Monday, February 29, 1836

As if we didn't have enough to worry about already—

Yesterday, just as people were quieting down about the Mexicans and starting to concentrate on their crops, a large herd of buffalo came by. There must have been three or four thousand of them. They passed within sight of our house but on the other side of the Brazos. They made a tremendous noise. We could not see the huge, woolly beasts very clearly—they were moving in a dark cloud of dust, which looked like a sandstorm blowing through.

Now, on top of Mexicans, we're worried about Comanches. They always follow the herd. For the next several nights, Uncle Peter will sleep in the stable with the horses to keep the Indians from stealing them.

Some time after nightfall, the last of the buffaloes must have passed by on their way to the coast. This morning, the prairie was so beat up it looked as if it had been plowed.

Tuesday, March 1, 1836

So it's happened. The battle is on. The Alamo is under attack. This shocking news came by messenger on horseback today. He brought a letter from Col. Travis, commander of the Texas forces at the Alamo:

> Commandcy of the Alamo—
> Bexar, Fby. 24th 1836—
> To the People of Texas &
> all Americans in the world—
> Fellow citizens & compatriots—
> I am besieged by a thousand
> or more of the Mexicans under
> Santa Anna—I have sustained
> a continual Bombardment &
> cannonade for 24 hours & have
> not lost a man—The enemy
> has demanded a surrender at
> discretion otherwise, the garrison
> are to be put to the sword, if

the fort is taken—I have answered
the demand with a cannon
shot, & our flag still waves
proudly from the walls—<u>I</u>
<u>shall never surrender or retreat</u>.
Then, I call on you in the
name of Liberty, of patriotism &
of everything dear to the American
character, to come to our aid,
with all dispatch—The enemy is
receiving reinforcements daily &
will no doubt increase to three or
four thousand in four or five days.
If this call is neglected, I am deter
mined to sustain myself as long as
possible & die like a soldier
who never forgets what is due to
his own honor & that of his
country—<u>Victory or Death</u>.

William Barret Travis
Lt. Col. Comdr.
P. S. The Lord is on our side—
When the enemy appeared in sight
we had not three bushels of corn—
We have since found in deserted
houses 80 or 90 bushels & got into
the walls 20 or 30 head of Beeves—
Travis

This letter has produced a great sensation in our colony. A great spirit has arisen to go to the aid of our fighting brothers at the Alamo. I shudder to imagine them facing an enemy ten to twenty times their number. Oh, dear God, bless my brother trapped in the Alamo.

The messenger and his horse were broken down, so Guy offered to carry Col. Travis's dispatch to the lower settlements so they could get their own troops ready. He galloped off at lightning speed. I could tell by how high he held his head that he was proud to carry a letter of such urgency and gallantry. Being a home guard does count.

Wednesday, March 2, 1836

It is bone-chilling cold. A cold front must have blown through as we slept, dropping the temperature near freezing.

People talk of nothing but war. There has been a great turnout among our able-bodied citizens to rein-force the Alamo men. It is not just the young men enrolling in the local militias. Even some of Father's friends with families—Messrs. Neal, Bell, and Dyer— have joined up.

With Father and some others away at the convention, and the militias soon to depart, only a handful of white men will remain in our settlement. Angus, being crippled, can't fight. Instead, he is temporarily filling in for Guy as home guard, while Guy relays the Travis letter downriver. And, of course, Mr. Shipman stayed home. He's much too old to fight.

Everyone is pitching in for the war effort. We stayed up half the night sewing shirts and knapsacks for our soldiers. Even Toby made a bag or two. Aunty Rachel and Milindy spent all day melting lead in a pot, dipping it up with a spoon, and molding bullets.

Thursday, March 3, 1836

Everything is chaos. Troops are drilling, preparing to leave for battle, refugees stumble by on foot, horse, or in carts, and, down at the landing, men load boats with guns and ammunition for the army. Couriers ride hither and yon, carrying secret dispatches to important military leaders. The air is charged with an odd mix of excitement and fear.

We stay busy to keep sane. Sister, Little Henrietta, Eliza, Stephen, and I are working in the fields alongside Uncle Peter, Milindy, Toby, and Aunty Rachel. It feels good to dig my fingers into the brownish red soil, making something grow. GM looks after Mother in the house, now confined to her bed, being so great with child.

I've asked around town about Prissy, but no one has seen her. I look at her empty bed and worry. I know I've said mean things about Prissy, but if I don't worry about her, then who will? Her mother is long dead and, according to Dr. Phelps, her father has gone off and joined the army, thinking Prissy is safely here with us.

Friday, March 4, 1836

Now we know the worst. Santa Anna has sent a second Mexican division, 1,000 troops under the command of General Urrea, into Texas. Urrea's forces are slashing their way up the coast toward our settlement. A few days ago, they marched into San Patricio after midnight, taking the small Texian unit under Col. Johnson by surprise. All fifty of those poor Texians were slaughtered.

If Urrea's army were to travel fast, it could be here in a little more than a week, especially if there is no Texian army to block it at Goliad. No one knows of the whereabouts of Urrea's army—or Fannin's. Did Fannin abandon Goliad and head west to San Antonio to reinforce the Alamo men?

Everything is a muddle. I'm not sure of anything

anymore. Should we stay, as Father insisted? Or, run, knowing now that our settlement truly is threatened?

Never in my fourteen years have I ever been so scared and confused. Rumor is that Santa Anna emptied the Mexican prisons to swell the size of his armies. That means his soldiers include murderers, rapists, and thieves. What if one of Santa Anna's divisions does indeed invade Columbia? Will they capture us? Kill us? Or—worse?

I lie in bed and worry about to whom to turn to for advice. Before the war, when I had night terrors, I could tiptoe downstairs and confide in Father or Mother. But I can't do that now. Father's away at the convention and, if I share my fears with Mother, she could lose the baby. And any upset makes GM's heart beat dangerously fast. And Sister's never any help. She just comes undone and cries, making things ten times worse.

If only Maggie lived closer. I'd even talk to Prissy at this point, if I knew where she was. Guy would know what to do. What's taking him so long, delivering that letter?

Only prayer calms me.

"Be a lamp unto my feet, Dear God," I pray, "direct my path and grant me strength to endure."

Saturday, March 5, 1836

We have had no news of any kind from the army. I wish Mac could get a letter to us, but I hear the Alamo is completely surrounded and couriers can seldom come and go.

Panic and fear are increasing. More men, women, and children are evacuating from the lower settlements now. On they go, one after another, through the woods, across the river, and across the prairie, seeming to have nothing in mind but going quickly eastward to the States, and safety.

My back aches from planting so many potatoes.

Sunday, March 6, 1836

Guy returned to Wood's Landing tonight—with Prissy! Sister and I were knitting in front of the fire when they came in. Prissy did not speak. When she saw us, she hid her face in her hands and ran upstairs, sobbing.

Guy took off his hat and sat down. He told of how he had ridden to Brazoria with the Travis letter, where immediately he was surrounded by a large crowd. After a copy of the letter was taken, he rode on downriver to his home at Peach Point. After getting a fresh horse, he rode on further to Velasco on the coast.

He crossed the Brazos there and reported to Capt. Poe, handing over the letter. It was from Capt. Poe that he learned that there were two prisoners at the fort—both of them Texians. They were the Baron and Prissy! The Baron had been caught smuggling 45 slaves (breaking Mexican law!) upriver on the *Shenandoah*, a boat reserved for evacuating Texas colonists. The Baron planned to sell the slaves and had no official permission to take the ferry. The Texian officials say he stole the ferry and—what's worse—endangered countless Texian lives. And Prissy was with him!

Oh! And to think that poor Milindy already knew the Baron's character. No wonder she dropped the Baron's calling card when the roses came. Had Milindy only been able to confide in me, we might have spared Prissy this shame.

Guy left the Baron to face justice, but managed to persuade the officials to release Prissy to his custody. The Baron—that rat! That explains Prissy's pearls. Now I understand. The Baron was seen in Columbia the night before Prissy went missing.

Wednesday, March 9, 1836

Finally—a long letter from Father:

> *Washington-on-the-Brazos*
> *6th March 1836*

My dear loved ones,

Forgive me for the delay in writing. This is the first time I have had to write to you with convenience.

When I arrived at the convention, I found my task as a delegate greatly changed. I was handed a copy of the most recent letter from Col. Travis. Santa Anna has invaded Texas. We are at war.

Although not all the delegates had yet arrived, those of us present knew what we had to do—draft a statement of Texas independence. We had to break all ties with Mexico officially.

In a drafty assembly hall, in freezing cold temperatures, we worked day and night until the declaration of independence was written and signed. Yes, our long national sweet dream is finally realized. We now live in the new, self-governing Republic of Texas.

We were split upon what to do next. Many wanted to adjourn and rush to the defense of our Alamo

*brethren. General Houston called this notion "folly"
and "treason" and beat the measure down. I have been
appointed to a commission charged with writing a set
of laws for our new country.*

*Today, the General bid us farewell. He has issued a
proclamation announcing the declaration of independence and calling on the citizens of Texas to rally,
as war is raging on the frontier. He has appointed
Gonzales as his headquarters. He hastened there, hoping many men will hear his call-to-arms and join his
army on its way to San Antonio.*

Pray for Mac. He is in great peril.

*I hope you will do your best, and I will do the same.
I must close. Do not be uneasy about me.*

> *Your affectionate husband*
> *and father,*
> *Josiah Wood*

*P.S. The General has made me captain of the
Columbia company. I have sent a man to Columbia to
organize my unit and march them to Gonzales. When
I am finished with my official duties here, I will find
the army and join the fight for liberty. Do not be
uneasy about me. God is always with me.*

> *I must close.*
> *Josiah*

Friday, March 11, 1836

Yet another letter from Father, and this one most disturbing.

A Texian courier has escaped through enemy lines at the Alamo with another letter addressed to the convention: Fannin's not coming! Although Travis has repeatedly sent him urgent appeals for help at the Alamo, Fannin ignores them. He never left Goliad! He's still holding that fort and refuses to budge.

So far, only 32 men from Gonzales have arrived to reinforce the Alamo men. Meanwhile, more Mexican troops arrive daily, encircling the Alamo on all sides, and bombarding its stone walls with heavy cannonade and howitzer shell. The enemy's numbers are estimated at between 1500 and 6,000 men. Col. Travis commands fewer than 200! Col. Travis beseeched the colonists to rush to his aid with reinforcements, ammunition, and provisions.

Poor Col. Travis! Oh, how I wish he could see outside the Alamo walls and how many men are rushing to help him. The Texas countryside swarms with men going west, shouldering muskets and rifles, marching in haste to help defend the Alamo.

The question is: will they reach there in time to save our men, our beloved Mac?

Saturday, March 12, 1836

Prissy has been teaching Little Henrietta and Eliza to play the piano. How she keeps them from fidgeting is beyond me. No one has pressed Prissy for an explanation as to why she ran off with the Baron—and she hasn't offered one either.

Sister's dying to ask, but Guy wants the incident hushed up. If word got out that Prissy was on a boat, unchaperoned with a man, it would bring dishonor to her family name.

The Baron better hope that Prissy's father doesn't hear about it. Being a blacksmith, Mr. Pruitt must be very strong. I wouldn't want his hands around my neck.

Sunday, March 13, 1836

Time lies heavy on our hands. Though it's the Sabbath, no camp meeting was scheduled for today. We could have used the distraction from our worrying.

Prissy suggested we hold our own camp meeting—inside the parlor. So we did. She was the pianist, I was the preacher, and Sister and Little Henrietta served the grape juice and the bread. We sang "O God, Our Help in Ages Past" three times.

Afterwards, we all felt much better, fortified on the inside, and closer to one another.

Friday, March 18, 1836

I was walking in the woods when the terrible news came. When I returned home, I found everyone gathered in the parlor. Among them was a visitor, our neighbor, Capt. Patton. All looked sad and talked but little.

Capt. Patton beckoned for me to come out of the doorway and take a seat. Then he told me why everyone wore long faces.

"The Alamo and its defenders have fallen," he said, eyes downcast. "All have perished."

The news came upon me like a clap of thunder. My brother Mac is dead.

Uncle Peter was all ready to drive the wagon to San Antonio to pick up Mac's body but Capt. Patton put an end to that.

"Peter, there is no body," he said. "Santa Anna had Mac's and all the others' remains burned to ashes."

When Mother heard this, she cried out, "Ohhh! My poor son! His body committed to the flames!" and collapsed in a faint. Uncle Peter carried her to her bed. We'd call for Dr. Phelps but he's away with the army now.

I thought of Mac's poor body, tossed into the heap upon a funeral pyre. What an evil brute this Santa Anna is. Civilized people allow the vanquished to bury their dead! Santa Anna has treated our men like common pirates. His soldiers burned their bodies like so much cordwood. We wonder if Father knows—if he will come home. We are so overcome with grief that we are no comfort to one another.

Sunday, March 20, 1836

None of us could rest until we did something for Mac. So, at sunset, all but Mother climbed the bluff to the family cemetery and held a memorial ceremony for him. We held hands and prayed, then Uncle Peter hammered a simple yet dignified wooden cross into the ground. Little Henrietta, Toby, and Eliza sprinkled rose petals around its base.

Now Mother has three children in heaven. I pray to God this child she is carrying may live. She is confined to her bed. Oh why can't Father be here? We need his strength.

Monday, March 21, 1836

The news is coming thicker and faster since the fall of the Alamo. General Houston and his small Texas army were forced to abandon their headquarters at Gonzales because a division of Santa Anna's army is in hot pursuit of them. They are currently encamped on the Colorado River. Unfortunately, when General Houston left Gonzales, he had to leave his cannons behind. He had no carts with which to transport them. He sunk them in the river, so that the big guns would not fall into the hands of the Mexicans.

The General has ordered all families living west of the Colorado to flee east. Those of us living east of the Colorado are still being asked to stay in our homes. General Houston will hold the Mexican forces at the Colorado and keep them from crossing into our settlement.

Tuesday, March 22, 1836

This morning, two men rode into our yard and pulled their guns on Uncle Peter. They demanded that he turn over all of our horses "for service in the army." Uncle Peter did as he was told and emptied the stables. Guy was off in Columbia at the time. Fortunately, he had ridden Beauty into town or she, too, would have been taken.

When Guy returned and learned what had happened, he shook his head. Those men were not special government agents, he said, but common horse thieves.

All our horses have been stolen. Now only Beauty remains.

Wednesday, March 23, 1836

We feel quite helpless with only one horse. Should we need to flee the Mexicans in a hurry, we can hitch up some oxen to pull our wagon. But once the wagon is loaded with provisions and bedding, there'll only be a little room inside for a few passengers. Some of us would have to flee on horseback. So Guy left this morning on a boat bound for Peach Point. He'll return shortly to bring us some horses on loan.

Mr. Pilgrim has closed up the school, and he, Eliza, and Stephen packed up all their belongings and, sadly, left with Guy for good.

Friday, March 25, 1836

Late

Guy rode in tonight with two horses for us. He rode his own horse, King, and is anxious to show him to me. It was too dark to visit the stables tonight, though. I guess I'll have to wake up very early if I'm going to see this favorite horse before Guy heads back home in the morning. I hate for him to leave again, but his family is abandoning Peach Point. "My stepfather feels the Mexicans are too close for comfort," he told us.

Guy urged us to join his family in fleeing overland. He said that many people in our colony are also fleeing. On his return trip here today, he passed through Brazoria, where he saw many of our neighbors boarding boats to take refuge on Galveston Island. He saw Maggie and her family board one such schooner, assisted by Angus McCoy.

We are wretched. All appears lost. We want to flee, but Mother refuses to budge. She insists upon hearing from Father first. She can't bear to leave not knowing where he is. Is he still at the convention in Washington-on-the-Brazos? Or did he join General Houston in the army? We haven't heard from him in two weeks.

Oh, I almost forgot something else Guy said. The Baron is out of jail. He's offering a $250 reward for the capture of Moss. Now Moss must flee Peach Point. Soon the entire countryside will be crawling with bounty hunters.

Saturday, March 26, 1836

Early this morning, while Guy was saddling up for his return to Peach Point, Milindy and I packed a special lunch for his journey. We hustled out to the gate to meet him and see this horse he's so fond of.

Imagine our surprise when Guy trotted up riding a milky-white mustang! Milindy's mouth dropped open.

"Lord, Miss Belle, would you just look at that! That's the horse I told you about!"

She said it was the very same white mustang the dark stranger had ridden the night he rescued me at Bailey's Prairie. Since that was the case, it could only mean one thing—Guy Bryan was my white knight!

As these ideas clicked through my brain at rapid speed, Guy was dismounting his horse and leading him over to where Milindy and I were standing, struck dumb. He dropped the reins and said to his horse, "*¡Quédate!*—Stay put!" with quite a merry twinkle in his eye.

"Belle," he said, gesturing toward his horse, "meet King; King, Belle." I reached out and stroked King's mane.

Then I fixed my gaze on Guy. "Now why didn't you tell me it was you who rescued me on Bailey's Prairie?" I asked, crossing my arms over my chest, miffed.

"Well, it's not as if I didn't drop you a couple of clues," he replied.

"Clues?" I asked, taking a step closer, and cocking my head to one side. "What clues?"

"Well, my Spanish for one. Then there's that jar of honey I brought you."

"What does a jar of honey have to do with rescuing me on Bailey's Prairie?" I asked, growing exasperated despite myself.

"Remember last November when you had to return to Bailey's Prairie in broad daylight? I believe you were dropping off a bag of bullets," he said.

"Hey!" I exclaimed. "You're not supposed to know about that!"

"Well, of course I'm supposed to know about that,"

he chuckled, "I'm the one who picks up the bullets! I've been picking up drops on Bailey's Prairie ever since this war began. That's what I was doing the night of your accident—and that's why I brought you that jar of honey when I first met you. I was dropping you a clue. Don't you get it?—honey—bees—bee tree?"

I had to admit that was clever. I punched his arm playfully. "All right—so you had me there. What else?"

"Do you remember that early Saturday morning we went riding? Didn't you wonder how I knew which bedroom window to throw pebbles at? How'd I know which room was yours? I hadn't ever been in your bedroom before—or—had I?"

I thought back. Well, of course, he had—that night he'd carried me in and laid me before the fire, sopping wet and unconscious.

I was sore. Guy had been having great fun at my expense.

He must have expected this because he had come prepared to soften me up. He walked over to King, dug into his saddlebag, and took out a box.

"Here," he said, shoving a wrapped gift into my hands. "I hope you can forgive me. I hated leaving you unconscious that night without even talking to your parents, but I was under strict orders not to reveal my presence on Bailey's Prairie that night to anyone. No hard feelings, okay?" The box was wrapped in shiny white paper and grandly tied up with a satin blue bow. I looked around to see if we were being observed. Milindy was nowhere in sight. She must have sneaked away to give us some privacy.

"Go ahead," he said, "open it."

I untied the ribbon and tore off the wrapping. I lifted the lid of the box. Tucked inside some tissue was an elegant, handheld, silver-framed mirror. Before I knew what I was doing, I had thrown my arms around his neck. "Oh, Guy, how beautiful!"

It was hard to watch him ride off. I thought about the last time I saw Mac. What if I never saw Guy again?

My stupidity amazes me. How could I have been attracted to the Baron when a fellow like Guy was walking this earth? What a fool I've been—grasping for coins instead of diamonds.

My white knight—I've finally found him—but now he's gone—

Oh, bother! There's so much I forgot to ask him about that night on Bailey's Prairie. Was he or was he not carrying a lantern? And, if he wasn't, then who was?

Palm Sunday, March 27, 1836

I know that we're not supposed to work on the Sabbath, but today, we just had to. If the Mexicans are coming, we're not about to leave our valuables lying around for them to steal.

So, without Mother's knowledge, we went to work to hide our treasures. We sank our crockery in the bottom land along Bell Creek. Then, out in the pasture, Uncle Peter placed two posts a considerable distance apart and buried over 100 bushels of potatoes, vegetables, and corn midway between them. Finally, we hauled books, silverware, and other valuables (my silver mirror) up to the peach bluff and buried them in the cemetery. We wore ourselves out, until we just dripped with perspiration in this warm and muggy spring air.

Monday, March 28, 1836

We don't believe what we've just heard. It just can't be true.

General Houston has retreated from the Colorado! He and his army are falling back to the Brazos!

How can this be? Now no army stands between us and the enemy. General Houston promised to hold the

Mexicans at the Colorado! Nothing will keep them from crossing the river into the settled country now. Uncle Peter said some Mexicans were spotted on Caney Creek—just a few miles from here.

General Houston has sent an agent to Columbia to guide us to safety. Everyone is packing, preparing to flee.

We hear that even our government officials are running from the advancing Mexican army. They've abandoned Washington-on-the-Brazos and fled to Harrisburg. Did Father go with them or join the army? How will we know?

Tuesday, March 29, 1836

You can imagine the relief we all felt when we saw Father ride up the lane today. Sister, Little Henrietta, and I ran to the gate. Father jumped off his horse and swept us up into his arms. We heard Mother cry from an upstairs window, "Josiah! You're home!"

He's home, but not for long. He's come to take us to safety, before he goes off to rejoin the army. The Mexicans will soon be at the Brazos, he says, where the Texas army is currently encamped.

He's not sending us to Galveston, where so many

neighbors and friends (including Maggie!) have taken refuge, but to Harrisburg.

"Galveston is out of the question," says Father. "Our scouts intercepted one of the enemy's communications. Santa Anna intends to occupy Galveston with a large army. Harrisburg is safer." And I was so sure Maggie was among the safe ones.

It's the first time we've seen Father since word of Mac's death. We took him up to the peach grove and showed him Mac's memorial. The sight of Father weeping was more than any of us could bear. We, too, broke down and cried. When will our grieving end?

Wednesday, March 30, 1836

The yard is covered with feathers. Aunty Rachel caught 24 grown chickens, dressed them, and put them in large washpots to boil. We'll need plenty of meat for our long journey to Harrisburg.

Thursday, March 31, 1836

General Urrea has conquered Goliad! Col. Fannin and his 400 men have surrendered! The Mexicans are marching toward Columbia!

We left home within an hour of getting this warning.

Uncle Peter hastily hitched up four oxen to the covered wagon. Aunty Rachel and Milindy gathered whatever bedding, clothes, and provisions they thought we should need and threw them in the wagon. Father tossed a feather mattress in and laid Mother on it. GM, Little Henrietta, and Toby climbed in next. Little Henrietta was clutching her cat, Domino.

Uncle Peter turned most of the cattle and hogs loose in the woods to forage for food while we are gone, but brought along a few in case we run out of food and need fresh meat. Aunty Rachel, Milindy, and Prissy's maid, Flo, will drive those few cows and pigs up the trail on foot. Uncle Peter, too, is walking, tending the oxen that pull our wagon. Thanks to Guy, Sister and Prissy have horses to ride. I'm riding Beauty, of course, and Father is leading our caravan on his horse as far as the ferry.

With the river too swollen to cross at Columbia, we have to go up to Old Fort at Richmond to catch the ferry. That's a good thirty miles north of home. When the twelve of us started out today, we were four in the wagon, four on foot, and four on horseback. We left home before noon in a cold and drizzling rain. The corn was thigh-high in our fields.

Leaving everything we have ever worked for is just too sad for words.

Friday, April 1, 1836

8 miles north of Columbia

Morning

Just now, while lying upon my bed of dry leaves, I was aroused from my slumber by clucking and gobbling. I looked up. We had encamped beneath a large roost of wild turkeys. The trees were filled with them. They are such tame and trusting birds. Mac used to hunt them with only a bow and arrow.

I saw that Uncle Peter had already kindled a fire and was boiling the coffee.

We're eight miles north of Columbia—where the road forks. The left fork leads to San Felipe; the right, to Richmond. Today, we'll strike the right fork to Richmond. We're traveling with five other planter families from Columbia and Brazoria, including the Pattons and the Varners.

Saturday, April 2, 1836

Our group of movers grows larger and larger by the hour. The whole country is fleeing from Santa Anna's troops.

Easter Sunday, April 3, 1836

South of Richmond

Noon

What a night of terror to usher in an Easter morn—

Yesterday was such a good day, too. We covered close to ten miles, putting ourselves within a day's ride of Richmond. Our progress was encouraging. Before nightfall, we turned a few paces aside from the road and pitched camp. I turned Beauty loose to graze in the tall grass. After a simple meal of dried beef and beans, I spread my saddle blanket upon a bed of dry grass Uncle Peter had cut for me with his knife, lay down, and fell fast asleep before the warm fire.

Along about midnight, I awoke—thoroughly chilled and wet. A piercing norther was sweeping over the prairie. It was bitterly cold. I gathered my blanket around me and scampered underneath the wagon, where I found I wasn't alone. Sister and Milindy were there, too. Soon, though, the water rose around us, and we had to crawl up into the wagon and join the other womenfolk. Father and Uncle Peter stayed outside with the livestock, to keep them from bolting.

Ten of us (plus a meowing cat) were squished in that

wagon. Hail began striking the canvas like rifle shot. All we could do was wait out the storm. The rest of the night, nobody slept a wink.

When daylight came, and with it, Easter, we resumed our journey—but slowly and painfully, as our limbs are so stiff and numb and the road has turned to slush. We're slogging through knee-deep mud, as thick as molasses. We'll be lucky to reach Richmond by tomorrow night—if pneumonia doesn't get us all first.

Monday, April 4, 1836

Still south of Richmond

Noon

At daybreak today, a most unusual man stumbled into our camp.

When I first saw him emerge from the woods, I thought he might have been a pirate. His face was as brown as an Indian's. His cap perched on his head like a turban—the brim had been ripped off. His hunting shirt was all tattered and blackened with smoke. What was left of his pants was held up by a leather belt, from which hung a tin cup and two long carving knives. He wore a knapsack on his back, to which were tied two dead, skinny chickens and one fat duck.

He'd smelled our breakfast cooking. Aunty Rachel

ladled up a plate of corn mush and handed it to him with a spoon. Milindy poured coffee in his tin cup. He squatted by the fire and we gathered around. We're always glad to meet a stranger. They bring news.

This stranger surprised us. He was no pirate. Despite his filthy appearance, he had a courtly manner. "Allow me to introduce myself," he said, bowing low at the waist. "I am John C. Duval. Last November, I came here from Kentucky with my brother, Burr—to help Texians throw off the Mexican yoke! Burr and I sailed from New Orleans on a schooner. We made straight for Goliad, where we joined Col. Fannin's company of men. We fought with Fannin," here he took a deep breath, "until the surrender." He swallowed spoonful after spoonful of corn mush, washing it down with great gulps of strong black coffee.

When he resumed speaking, his face had saddened. "But Burr's dead now, you know, and Fannin and his bunch and the New Orleans Greys, too—all of them dead, except for me and maybe a few others lucky enough to escape the Mexican firing squads."

We were stunned.

"Mexican firing squads?" exclaimed Father, jumping to his feet. "Do you mean to tell me that Col. Fannin and his men are dead?"

Mr. Duval nodded.

"But Col. Fannin and General Urrea had agreed to terms," cried Father, in disbelief. "Fannin would turn over the guns and surrender if Urrea would treat Fannin's men as prisoners of war and return them to the United States. Urrea assured him there'd be no loss of life upon surrender!"

"Yes, that's what was supposed to happen," replied Mr. Duval. "But it didn't. We were tricked. That Santa Anna is devious—he doesn't play by the rules of civilized governments."

He explained. "On the morning of March 27, Palm Sunday, a Mexican officer came to us at the fort in Goliad where we were imprisoned, and ordered us to get ready for a march. He said we were to be 'liberated' and put on a boat to New Orleans.

"Well, as you can imagine, this was joyful news to us. We did not suspect foul play—although we should have. Some Mexican women, standing near the entrance of the fort, hinted at the trouble to come, had we paid attention. As four hundred of us filed out the gates past the women, they sighed, shook their heads sadly, and called us *pobrecitos*. That means 'poor fellows' in Spanish.

"Anyway, we were divided into three separate groups, double file, and marched out under strong guard. Each of these three groups was sent in a different direction. That did seem odd to me, to be sent off in three different directions—we were all supposedly headed to the same place—to Copano Bay—to board a boat.

"My group took the road to San Antonio. We were about a mile above Goliad when one of our Mexican guards cried "Halt!" It was then that I heard heavy musket fire coming from the directions taken by the other two groups. A Texian near me shouted, 'Boys! They're going to shoot us!' At that same instant, I heard the clicking of musket locks all along the Mexican line behind us. I turned to look, and, as I did, the Mexicans fired upon us, killing at once probably one hundred of the one hundred and fifty of us."

But Mr. Duval wasn't shot. He took off running, the Mexican guards hot on his heels. When he reached the banks of the San Antonio River, he dove in and swam underwater for his life. The swift current carried him downstream while bullets pattered in the water over his head. He's been on the run ever since, dodging Mexican soldiers by hiding in canebrakes and deserted cabins. He says it's not safe anywhere—the whole countryside is crawling with small units of armed Mexicans.

We tried to convince him to join our traveling party,

but he was intent upon resuming his independent journey. Upon finishing his meal, he thanked us effusively and bowed. Bidding us adieu, he went on his lonely, mysterious way.

Father shook his head and looked at the ground. "Two massacres in one month. The Alamo men—massacred. The Goliad men—massacred. Now only one Texian army stands between us and destruction—and that unhappy burden, my dears, rests with General Samuel Houston."

In a wood on the banks of the Brazos River, below Richmond

Nightfall

Complete exhaustion caused us to halt for the day— short of our goal. We're encamped in the woods bordering the Brazos. We'll spend the night in this streak of timber, where the trees shield us somewhat from the rain. What miserable, sopping cold.

We had hoped to make it all the way to Richmond today, but this constant rain prevented it. We managed to cover only six miles. Our wagon got stuck in the bottomless black mud at least six times!

To lighten the load, Father lifted Mother onto Beauty

with me, and GM and Sister doubled up. Even then, once, the oxen fell into a bog so deep that they turned the wagon upside down, spilling its cargo into the soft mud, where it was easy to sink out of sight. This Toby and Little Henrietta proceeded to do, as they had been tossed out with the cargo. Milindy, Prissy, and I jumped in to rescue the mud-strangled ones, while Father and Uncle Peter recovered our goods. Then, using ropes and horses, we pulled wagon and oxen out of the sticky mess. This took most of the afternoon. By then, we were all so muddy it was almost impossible to tell one of us from the other. We counted to be sure all twelve of us were present before trudging onward.

All that pulling and lifting and carrying makes my arms and legs throb with pain. My head is pounding. But the campsite is quiet. I must draw comfort from the protective circle of wagons and a dozen winking fires—

Tuesday, April 5, 1836

Arrival at Richmond

For fourteen years I've lived on the Brazos. I've fished in it, waded in it, and sailed its gentle green waters. Never, though, have I seen it look like this—a raging torrent, wide and overflowing its banks, cluttered with dead trees, spinning with whirlpools, and foaming with rapids. It seems to boil. My heart sank to see it so. How are we ever going to cross such a dangerous watercourse?

I can't believe the crowd of people waiting here at Richmond. Over a hundred families are ahead of us to cross the river.

Capt. Martin and his picket guard are in charge of the ferry. They take the cattle over first and then come back for the people. It's all done very slowly, with much difficulty, and at great risk of drowning. It'll take days before it's our turn. How will the Mexicans not get us first?

I was staring at the huge crowd of waiting people, filling with fear and just about to cry, when I heard Prissy's voice. She took me gently by the arm.

"Belle," she said, wheeling me around, "do you see that group of refugees over there?" She pointed out a cluster of women and children milling around wagons and fires. They, too, were waiting to cross. Some of the women rested on the ground while others moved about, barefoot and muddy, thin and bent, stirring kettles, chopping wood, stoking the fire, with young, scared-looking children clinging to their skirts. The women's movements were sad, heavy, and slow.

Their vehicles were clumsy homemade truck carts pulled by scrawny oxen. I scanned their campsite. They slept out in the open. Where, I wondered, were their strong men, their sturdy horses?

"Who are they?" I asked Prissy.

"They are the widows and orphans of the Alamo. They come from Gonzales. Their men died fighting at the Alamo. After the Alamo fell, they fled Gonzales with General Houston and his army. The General ordered that their homes be burned to the ground, so that nothing might be left for the Mexican army to enjoy."

I tucked my head and blinked back stinging tears. Those poor people. We had lost Mac at the Alamo, but we still had Father and Guy, and Uncle Peter. The Gonzales refugees had no time to rescue belongings or any way to carry them. They have nothing and no one to return to.

I gazed at our campsite—truly seeing it perhaps for the very first time—our fine horses, our covered wagon, our faithful servants, our brave men. To the widows and orphans of the Alamo, we must look like grandees, to have so much.

Thursday, April 7, 1836

Still at Richmond

Late

Santa Anna has been spotted within a day's ride north of here! To wait for the ferry is to die.

Even though it's dark, axes are ringing through the bottomland of the Brazos. Everyone's building rafts. We just have to get across this wild river! Father and the other men traveling in our party are working some distance from camp, on the steep and slippery riverbank, cutting down elm and cypress to make us a raft. The raft has to be put together in the water.

They'll be up all night in this cold rain, working by torchlight. Father left Uncle Peter in charge of our camp. He's guarding all the women and children until morning. Hopefully, by then, the raft will be ready.

I don't think anyone will get much sleep tonight. Besides the axes ringing through the woods, there's another sound keeping us awake. It's the sound of children coughing.

Sickness has broken out in camp.

Saturday, April 9, 1836

It took two unbelievable days to get our party across the river. Everyone in the whole camp was trying to cross at once. It was almost a riot. The river was very dangerous. The current tried to push our raft downstream to the Gulf of Mexico. To keep the raft from being swept away, Father and the other men had to rig up a cable, like a ferry, to pull the raft back and forth for new loads. We had to take the wagons and carts apart to carry them across. All our bedding and clothes are completely soaked. Fortunately, we (animals included) crossed safely.

But not every creature was so lucky. One woman was so desperate to escape Santa Anna, she tried to cross the Brazos on her horse. Foolishly she spurred him on, until he plunged into the swift waters and made for the opposite bank.

At first, we thought he just might make it. Prissy and I ran down the bank to the water's edge to join a group of women shouting encouragement to the horse. But the water quickly rose over the horse's belly and swept him off his feet.

We watched helplessly as the valiant horse fought wildly against that current. But it was no use. The force of the water was too much for him. In just seconds, that poor, lovely, brave horse and his rider were swept downriver and sucked under. We strained to see them resurface, but they never did.

Sunday, April 10, 1836

On the Harrisburg Road

Father and the other men in his Columbia Volunteers left to go find the army. Then, after waving goodbye to Father, we, too, set out, with the thousands of other women, children, and Negroes running from the Mexicans, and headed east into the wilderness. After crossing Oyster Creek, we will follow the high ground between Bray's and Sims Bayous and into Harrisburg, some thirty miles. If we can just stay ahead of the Mexicans and reach Harrisburg, we'll be safe. I wonder which direction Guy and his family are headed. I pray they are well.

I've never seen such a cold and rainy spring.

Monday, April 11, 1836

Still on the Harrisburg Road

This prairie is covered with water. I've lost count how many times our wagon bogged in the mud today. Was it five times, or six? Over and over, Uncle Peter cracked his whip in the air and called to the oxen in his loudest voice, "Rise, Buck and Ball, and do your best!" At one point, the oxen were mired so badly, they lay on their sides, stuck in the mud, poking their nostrils out to breathe. I thought many times I should be drowned, Beauty sinking with me almost out of sight. In many places, the water is up to her saddle skirts.

All color has been washed from our clothes by this constant rain. Clouds of mosquitoes pursue us on our endless journey through mud and water, biting us until we itch and bleed. Nothing is ever dry or warm. Every kind of illness has broken out among us—measles, the ague, whooping cough, pneumonia. I am worried about Little Henrietta's runny nose—children are dying!

Today we watched a woman bury her baby girl, but the grave was so watery that her limp little body stayed down for scarcely a moment before it bobbed back up to the surface.

Tuesday, April 12, 1836

East of Stafford's Point Plantation

It took every bit of yesterday just to cross Oyster Creek. All day long, ragged refugees waded back and forth across the creek, picking up loved ones and taking them to the other side. They carried their children atop their shoulders and their old people in their arms.

At day's end, we were amazed to find a high and dry mound near a small stream. We made camp for the night. While we dried ourselves by the fire, Uncle Peter and Joe, Col. Varner's Negro, went off into the woods to hunt. They shot some wild turkeys. In no time, they had the giant birds roasting on a spit over the fire, the grease dripping and popping as it hit the burning hot coals. Aunty Rachel and Flo baked some Johnnycake and sweet potatoes in the ashes of the campfire.

The food smelled delicious. We were starved. Sister said a short grace. Prissy passed me the pitcher of molasses. I was busily dribbling circles of molasses on my cornbread, my mouth watering for that first sweet, crunchy bite, when I heard something that made the hair stand up on the back of my neck. I dropped the pitcher, spilling the molasses in the dirt. It was the howl of a wolf.

We got quiet and listened. A second wolf took up the howl—then a third and a fourth and so on until soon the whole countryside was howling with wolves. They must have smelled our food cooking. The howls got nearer and nearer. They drew so near we could soon see the pack prowling the edges of our campsite. Those wolves were big and black. We huddled closer to the fire.

What could we do? We threw all our food to them and still they wouldn't go away. We were surrounded by wolves and water. I was terrified—I couldn't move.

But not Uncle Peter. He directed Joe and some of the Negro boys traveling with us to gather as much dead wood as they could find.

"Pile it high upon the fire," he said to them when they returned with armloads of wood. The boys piled log upon log until that flame grew into a mighty bonfire. It glowed as bright as day around us.

But even that giant fire couldn't scare away those wolves. All that long night, Uncle Peter, Joe, and some of the other fellows stood guard. When the wolves would begin to howl and try to advance into our camp, one of the Negroes would hurl a piece of burning wood at them. For a while, the wolves would go silent and retreat into the shadows. But then they'd start closing in on us again. Eventually, we all began throwing fire-brands at them. Finally, along towards daylight, their howling ceased. They must have given up and slunk away. I dozed off close to dawn.

The whole experience must have been too much for GM. All day long, she has been talking out of her head. She says crazy things like, "Let's go bring in the cotton."

Wednesday, April 13, 1836

West of Harrisburg

Little Henrietta woke up with a head as hot as a frying pan, pink spots behind her ears, and sore eyes. "Measles," announced Prissy, deadly serious.

Mother is worried sick and wants to help, but she has her hands full with GM, who is still mumbling strange things and becoming more and more agitated. So before we broke camp this morning, Prissy climbed up into the wagon to be with Little Henrietta, whom she adores, and gladly volunteered to be her nurse. Prissy has already managed to get her little patient to sip some of Aunty Rachel's healing oakbark tea.

Oh, I hope the tea helps. Little Henrietta just has to get better. She just can't die! If we could only stop and rest. But we can't. We must press on to Harrisburg. Now the oxen must pull five people in the wagon (plus the cat, Domino—Toby's taking care of her now).

Sister's no help to anyone. She just rides and pouts. She doesn't appreciate how good she has it. She could take a lesson or two from Uncle Peter, Flo, and Aunty Rachel. If they are weary of walking and tending the stock animals, we'll never know it. They just trudge on. It's beneath their dignity to whine.

Milindy is riding Prissy's horse now. She and I have made ourselves useful by galloping up the trail ahead of the others. Uncle Peter asked us to scout for tree stumps jutting out of the mud. A broken axle could set us back a whole afternoon.

Our cows, horses, and pigs have grown positively fat, grazing on all this nourishing spring grass that greens up the prairie. What a blessing that the animals grow stronger as we grow more needy. We would be completely helpless out in the wilderness without our sturdy oxen to pull us and healthy horses to ride.

Deserters from our army keep passing us on foot and on horseback. They bring news. Their latest report is that General Houston and what is left of our army have crossed the Brazos on the steamboat the *Yellow Stone*. They are now on the march to Harrisburg.

Though rumors fly right and left, we haven't a clue where the Mexican army really is.

These Texian deserters are full of excuses as to why they ran out on our army in its hour of greatest need. They say they lost faith in General Houston as a commander because he ordered a retreat from the Mexicans. They say they want the General to stop running, to meet Santa Anna on a battlefield, and to fight. Well, how is General Houston supposed to stage a battle if his army keeps deserting?

These deserters are nothing but liars and cowards. They're the ones scared of battle, not the General. When General Houston is ready, he'll make a stand and fight. They'll see. I recall how eager Guy was to join the army. I miss him.

When the deserters pass by, we mock them by calling out: "Run! Run! Run for your lives! Santa Anna is chasing you!" Then we laugh with scorn as they skitter down the road like shadows.

Thursday, April 14, 1836

Arrival at Harrisburg

We are still in shock. We arrived at Harrisburg today to find it almost deserted. The citizens fled yesterday as did President Burnet and his cabinet. There is no refuge for us here. The citizens fled because they learned the awful truth before we did—that Santa Anna and his army crossed the Brazos right behind us and will march into Harrisburg tomorrow.

Our plans are shot to bits. We must push on—but where? For now, we're encamped north of Harrisburg, in the sandy pines on Buffalo Bayou, trying to decide.

Mother looks so pale. I pray she doesn't fall ill—especially with this baby coming. She is so frail. What if she, too, gets the measles? What would happen to the baby?

Nightfall

Rain! Rain! Rain! Every night is the same, my clothes and feet drenched. I know I should be grateful to dry them by the campfire, but I don't know how much longer I can bear this.

Finally, Little Henrietta's fever is going down, thanks to Prissy's loving care. I am starting to understand Prissy better. Flo told Milindy why she ran off with the Baron. She thought the Baron might marry her. Her father had been pressuring her to find a husband and move out of his house.

Nobody's making me marry anybody I don't want

to. I can open a school. Mr. Pilgrim told me I'd make a great teacher.

Mother's back is aching. That baby is long overdue. How I wish it would be born.

GM's quieter now, drifting in and out of sleep. I don't know if that's good or bad. She seems to have lost all sense of time or place. She keeps calling me Mary Sue Mudd, the name of her best friend from childhood back in the East. Mary Sue is long since dead.

"Mary Sue?" she asks me, "do you still live in that pretty white house on the corner?"

I humor her and say, "Yes," which settles her down for a while. She falls back to sleep. But when she wakes up, she starts it up again, asking me the same question over and over.

Friday, April 15, 1836

Encamped north, on Buffalo Bayou

The group we were traveling with has split up. Some families chose to head for Galveston, where we now know President Burnet and the cabinet have taken refuge, but we're not, even though that's probably where Guy is. Prissy—Priscilla, I mean—and I put our heads together today and made a decision for our group. We're not going to Galveston because we can't take our goods, our stock, and our Negroes with us on the boat. Instead, we'll continue overland, taking the old Lynchburg Road east toward the U.S. border, where American troops are waiting.

We'll have to cross three more (difficult) rivers and dangerous Indian territory. But we must continue eastward. To stay here is to face certain death. Santa Anna will be here any minute.

I'm tired of living on the road, eating wild meat and blackberries, and bathing in creeks and ponds. I dream of returning to my old life, a life of rocking and knitting in front of a roaring fire, soaking in a steaming hot tub, and collapsing into a feather bed at bedtime. And yet, at the same time, I really don't care a bit about that old life right now. All I really care about now is whether my loved ones are going to make it through this alive.

Oh, how much longer before this cruel war is over and we're safely back home, on our land?

Saturday, April 16, 1836

Still encamped north of Harrisburg on Buffalo Bayou

Although the sun went down hours ago, I can almost write without lamplight. That's because, to the southeast of our camp, the sky glows bright red with flames. It's the town of Harrisburg. It's burning. Santa Anna and his army had it torched. The dictator is taking out his anger on Harrisburg. He must have been really mad when, instead of capturing President Burnet and his men there as he had expected, he found the whole place abandoned. That means they must have burned Columbia, too, and our home with it—

The Mexican army is encamped three miles below here. This knowledge has produced fresh panic among the movers. Almost everyone is frantic to escape. Although it's late, many are packing up and running into the night. They're whipping up their horses and flurrying away as fast as they can.

We're staying here, though, for the night. When we made camp, Uncle Peter, as usual, unwrapped his tinderbox to light a fire. We were shivering with cold and wet and could not wait to warm ourselves by the fire. But Aunty Rachel stopped Uncle Peter before he could ignite his tinder. She said a campfire would betray our position to the Mexicans. So we had cold beef and cold cornbread for supper, plus some wild onions Toby picked in the prairie. Before turning our oxen loose to graze, we muffled their bells, again, so as not to alert the Mexicans to our presence.

Sunday, April 17, 1836

On the Lynchburg Road

We nearly froze to death last night, sleeping in the open in a cold drizzle without a fire. Although we bundled Little Henrietta up and tucked her in the wagon, she awoke with a nagging cough. Prissy says it just might be pneumonia. Mother now is coughing.

About noon, we crossed Vince's Bridge with the multitude of fleeing people. Behind us in the distance we could see smoke rising above what was once Harrisburg.

As we traveled eastward, we received two (false) reports that the enemy was rapidly approaching. It produced a near stampede among the movers. We had to veer off the road to avoid being trampled by people rushing up from the rear of the line.

To lighten their loads and move faster, these panicky people are throwing out all kinds of things from their wagons. Miles and miles of countryside are littered with their cast-off belongings. Today we passed a site where, for hundreds of yards, the prairie was white with feathers emptied out of mattresses.

We are passing countless abandoned campsites. In one spot stood an open trunk from which some articles had been hastily snatched. A few feet away, a mirror hung from a tree. Below the mirror sat a three-legged stool. I figure some man had been sitting on that stool, looking in the mirror, and having his morning shave when the false alarm was sounded and he fled, still lathered up.

Aunty Rachel urged us to remain calm and not copy the panicky people. "Those crazy things! What they be thinking? Throwing out the very things they need to survive! Fools! They might as well be killed as to starve to death. What good can they expect to come to them from throwing away their clothes and sacks of beans and flour? Humph."

With the greatest speed (for a loaded wagon), we, too, are trying to reach the San Jacinto River. Uncle Peter heard that the river is supposed to have a gentle current, that you can throw a stick into it and not detect its movement. If so, it should be an easy crossing. After that, we'll follow this muddy ribbon of road until we get to the town of Liberty on the Trinity. We'll continue until we cross the Neches River before finally reaching the Sabine—and safety.

This prairie is full of water and quicksand. I've lost count of the days, and the nights, it's been raining. Has it been forty yet? I'm so tired. I fell asleep riding Beauty today and almost fell off.

Monday, April 18, 1836

At the San Jacinto River

We arrived here last night and found the San Jacinto up to the top of its banks and running rapid. Fully five thousand people were waiting to cross and there's only one ferry.

I saw at once the impossibility of the situation. A lump formed in my throat. By the time it is our turn to cross, the Mexicans will be upon us. There must be some way out of this trap.

We've made camp under some oaks dripping with gray moss. Behind us is Buffalo Bayou. To the front of us lies a low, flat prairie that extends for nearly a mile. To our left lies a marsh bordering the San Jacinto River. On the other side of the river is a scattering of unpainted houses that make up the little town of Lynchburg.

Mother has the fever. Aunty Rachel is with her now. We have no doctor, no medicine. All we can do is pray that God watches over us and keeps Mother and her unborn baby alive.

Tuesday, April 19, 1836

Still waiting to cross the San Jacinto

Several times during the night, I was roused by a loud racket. It came from a bamboo thicket on the edge of the marsh. The bamboo popped and cracked as if a heavy wagon were hurtling through it. This morning, I went to investigate. In the soft ooze of the lagoon, I found a great many bear tracks.

Still waiting to cross. The strange days and nights go on.

Late afternoon, east of the San Jacinto!

We have finally had a bit of luck. We have crossed the river. Some very clever Yankees got us across. They felled and peeled two very tall pine trees, then laid them across the river to form a makeshift bridge. They set our wagon on the trees and pulled it across with a rope. Ours was one of seventy-five loaded wagons pulled over this afternoon. When we were crossing, a gust of wind knocked my bonnet into the water, which carried it swiftly downstream. That was my only bonnet. Now I must cover my head with an old tablecloth. I'm glad Guy can't see me now.

I'm so weary I can barely keep my eyes open. I'm glad we stopped for a bit; I was afraid of falling off Beauty. My knuckles are white from holding the reins in a death grip. But I must stay on my mount and help Uncle Peter scout for a campsite. With three of us ill, we strong ones must hold on. Mother's fever still hasn't broken and GM sleeps all the time. Aunty Rachel's about to drop from tending to them, night and day. I wish I could do more to help her.

We have news of our army. They're marching toward the San Jacinto! This morning, General Houston and a force of nine hundred men crossed Buffalo Bayou. At this very minute, they're on the same prairie we just left. Could Father be with them?

Tomorrow we start for Liberty.

Wednesday, April 20, 1836

A few miles off the Liberty Road

Night

We were within six miles from the nearest water and timber for an encampment when Mother's labor pains started. We needed to find some shelter with a dry place to lay her. This damp cold is about to kill her and the baby both. Mother's skin is ghostly white.

Fortunately, I remembered seeing a sign on a fence a half-mile back down the road that said, "Leal a

Mexico." Having learned some Spanish from Guy, I was able to translate it. It meant "Loyal to Mexico."

I figured that property enclosed by a fence might indicate someone living there—in a house. We badly needed to get Mother under a roof—and into a bed. We split from our group of movers, turned our wagon, horses, and animals around, and headed back the way we had come.

We had no problem finding the fence with the Spanish sign. We followed that fence for another half a mile when our attention was drawn to the barking of a dog coming from some woods on the property. We searched until we found a wide gate through which we entered the property. We continued on our course, following the incessant barking on into the woods. Every minute, the barking grew louder and nearer and Mother's pains grew sharper and closer together.

Blessedly soon, we came within sight of the dog. She was a friendly little black thing. She ran up to greet us, tail wagging, and escorted us to a wooden cabin nestled under some tall, spreading trees.

The front door of the cabin was wide open. No one was home. Evidently, even Texians who claimed to be Mexican loyalists were taking no chances of meeting up with the impulsively cruel Santa Anna. News of the slaughters at the Alamo and Goliad had caused even these Mexican loyalists to abandon their land and flee like us "rebels."

Uncle Peter carried Mother into one of the beds. GM was asleep, so Prissy and I put her in another bed in an adjoining room. Sister was sobbing, so we asked her to go outside. Then we got ready for the childbirth. Toby and Little Henrietta gathered wood and Uncle Peter built a fire in the fireplace. Aunty Rachel, Prissy, and Flo found sheets, towels, and blankets. I helped Milindy fill a big kettle with well water and hang it over the fire. Once the water was boiling, Milindy, Aunty Rachel, and Flo hurriedly gathered their supplies and disappeared into Mother's room, slamming the door, leaving Prissy and me to tend to the little ones.

While we waited nervously, we snooped around. Inside the cabin, everything remained just as the family had left it. We found food on the table; German books on the shelves; long smoking pipes on racks; and trunks filled with neatly folded clothes (and pretty, lacy bibi bonnets!). Out back was a crib stuffed with corn, potatoes, and pumpkin, and a smokehouse with at least a thousand pounds of sausage. In a shed, we also found a barrel of brown sugar and half a sack of coffee. Chickens and ducks ran throughout the yard, which, no doubt, had been protected from varmints by the watchful dog.

Cruel as it may sound, I breathed a sigh of relief every time I heard a moan or a scream come from that birthing room. In that way, I knew that my mother was still alive.

As Little Henrietta is feeling better, Priscilla and Sister took her down to the creek to play fetch with the dog we call Blackie. But I wanted to stay close to the cabin. I waited on the front porch with Domino curled up in my lap and waited.

It was twilight when I heard a terrific high-pitched wail come from the birthing room. The baby was born.

The others down at the creek heard it, too, and rushed back. It seemed an eternity before Aunty Rachel appeared in the doorway. She was holding a tiny bundle.

"Aren't you going to greet your new baby brother?" she asked the three of us girls with a wink for Priscilla. Her shiny face beamed with delight. She held the baby out for us to see more closely. His little face was all pinched and purple-red.

A baby boy! I have a brother again! I made Aunty Rachel unwrap him completely so I could count his arms, legs, toes, and fingers to see he was all in one piece. He is. He has black hair that sticks straight up like an Indian papoose's.

"And . . . Mother?" I asked, trying to get around Aunty Rachel's ample body to peek in and see her. I could tell by her face that Mother was all right, but I had to hear her say it.

Aunty Rachel blocked the doorway. "What you thinking, child? Your sainted mother don't need no visitors just now! Don't you know she's just plain wore out?"

Wore out. What blessed words.

What a wonderful feeling to be happy again. It has been so long since we've smiled and laughed and kicked up our heels. In celebration, Uncle Peter took one of the long German pipes down from the rack, filled it with tobacco, and gave it to Aunty Rachel to smoke.

We realized we were starved—and there was so much food to choose from. Our servants badly needed a break so Sister, Priscilla, and I cooked everyone a first-rate meal. For the first time since we left Wood's Landing, Little Henrietta showed a healthy appetite. She mopped up every last drop of brown gravy on her plate with her second wheat biscuit.

It was a marvelous occasion. If only GM had been well enough to embrace her new grandson and Father and Mac and Guy could have been here. I'll take the baby in to see GM in the morning.

There are several luscious beds in this cabin and I

have collapsed into one of them. After writing this last sentence, I plan to blow out the candle and fall into a preciously deep sleep.

Thursday, April 21, 1836

Still a few miles off the Liberty Road, at the abandoned German farmhouse

About midmorning, GM had not come out for breakfast so I went to check on her. I took the baby with me. When I entered her room, she was still in bed. I leaned over and kissed her. But she didn't stir. "GM?" I said, shaking her gently by the shoulder. "GM?" I asked again more insistently. But she still didn't respond. That got me really scared. "Aunty Rachel!" I screamed, alarming the baby I was holding, who began to cry. Aunty Rachel came running.

She bent over GM, took up her wrist, then laid two fingers against GM's throat. Slowly Aunty Rachel straightened herself. With tears streaking her face, she lifted the bed sheet and covered GM's still face.

I feel like someone has punched a giant hole in my heart. GM is gone. My sweet, funny GM. Words cannot express how dreadfully my heart aches.

Evening

Just this afternoon, we heard the sound of big guns firing. The cannonade and rifle shot came from the southwest—from the direction of the San Jacinto, the river we crossed only two days ago. The battle raged for less than half an hour before the guns went silent.

We imagine the worst has finally happened—the last Texian army has been wiped out, massacred, by the Mexicans. This just has to be the case. That cannonade couldn't have come from our side. General Houston doesn't even have any cannons. He abandoned them in Gonzales.

We are wretched with worry. Try as I may, I cannot fight the image of Father lying on the battlefield dying—blood spilling from the hole a musket ball has made in his chest—and no one there to comfort him.

We cannot delay. We must run even though it's growing dark and Mother is still so fragile. Having defeated the last of the Texian armies, the Mexican army will soon be on the march again. And this time, they'll be chasing Texian colonists. They'll be after our blood.

We regret that we have to leave GM's body here on someone else's land. We buried her beneath an old persimmon tree, behind the wooden cabin. We haven't told Mother of GM's passing yet. With Mother's health so feeble and her fever still high, the shock might be too much. We're letting her sleep for now, while Flo minds the baby. Sooner or later, though I cannot bear to think of it, Mother will awaken enough to miss GM.

We're packed and ready to go but, before leaving this place, I must scribble a hasty note of thanks to the absent owners. We have eaten their food, slept in their beds, and smoked their tobacco. Also, I must explain the newly dug grave.

It would be so easy for me to take one of the calico sunbonnets I found in a trunk inside to replace this old tablecloth I'm wearing on my head, but I just don't feel good about "borrowing" anything not absolutely necessary from these unwittingly kind folks.

I thought long and hard about whether or not to take Blackie along with us when we leave. I'm quite fond of her now; we all are. She fits right in. She gets along great with Domino and doesn't spook the cattle. But I decided not to take her. It would be too sad for her owners to return and find her missing. Anyway, what would the chickens and ducks do without Blackie around to guard them?

I must close and write my note of thanks—we've no more time to waste.

First Mac, then GM, and now Father—gone. When this is all over, will I have any tears left?

Saturday, April 23, 1836

Once again on the Liberty Road

Morning

Mother has received the news of GM's passing with amazing calm. She hugs her new baby to her chest. I pray the baby will keep her so busy and so happy that she has no time to dwell on sad things. Mother is still ill with fever.

Late afternoon

We had just crossed Cedar Bayou, heading east for Liberty, when we heard, way off behind us in the winding line of runaways, a muffled but persistent noise. As I strained to see where it was coming from, the noise grew louder. At length, I could see a man on horseback, waving his hat and shouting something I could not make out. As he passed along the swaying line of people, they shouted and jumped about, throwing up hats and bonnets and dancing in the lane.

It seemed like forever before the horseman galloped

within earshot of our wagon. His horse was all covered with foam. "Turn back! Turn back! No danger! No danger!" he cried hoarsely. "The Texians have captured Santa Anna and his army!"

At first we did not believe him. We have heard so many false reports. But one of our party recognized the rider and knows he can be trusted. So it's true. We have victory! We've defeated the Mexican army! Santa Anna has been captured. When we heard that the Dictator was a prisoner, we knew we had won not just a battle, but the war itself.

Never had I seen such rejoicing! All along that road between the San Jacinto and the Trinity—as far as I could see—there was nothing but hugging, kissing, and weeping.

Our information is sketchy. We know that the battle at San Jacinto lasted but a short while, under half an hour, and that our soldiers were magnificent, charging the battlefield with cries of "Remember the Alamo! Remember Goliad!" What I can't figure out is how our side won without using cannons.

I tremble to believe it. They say that fewer than ten Texians lost their lives. Can it be? Dare I pray that Father is still alive, that our neighbors and Mr. Pruitt may also be among the survivors?

Today is our first free day as the Republic of Texas. The independence we declared over a month ago is at last a reality.

Sunday, April 24, 1836

Heading back westward toward the San Jacinto River

My new baby brother is so cute. Little Henrietta is feeling much better. This morning, Mother's head is not hot anymore. And we have victory. Things are looking up.

Monday, April 25, 1836

Back at the San Jacinto prairie, on the battlefield

Late afternoon

We crossed the San Jacinto River this morning. Angus McCoy was at the ferry when we landed, and it was like seeing a brother. I have gravely misjudged him. He is no coward. He fought in the battle here on Thursday, despite his crippled arm.

He escorted us to the battlefield. Both armies are camped on opposite sides of the prairie. The Texian army pitched their tents in the very same mossy oak grove (on the Bayou) where our family encamped just a few days ago, near the lagoon with the bear tracks.

We were wrong about the cannons. The Texians did have some—two six-pounders. According to Angus, the big guns arrived just in time for the battle, sent by boat from the citizens of Cincinnati to aid our cause. Our soldiers had no cannon balls, so they loaded the guns with whatever they could find for shot, tossing in handfuls of musket balls, broken glass, and horseshoes. The cannon fire threw the Mexicans into confusion and allowed our infantry to overrun them. Our army has affectionately named the two cannons the Twin Sisters.

Angus took us to see Father, who is very much alive, but dirty and ragged. His hair is shaggy, and he's grown a beard! He wept when he heard of GM's passing. He embraced Little Henrietta, who actually has roses in her cheeks again. When we laid his new son in his arms, Father wept some more. It does my heart good to see him. I can't hug him enough. He was aghast to see how thin Mother has become.

Priscilla's father, Mr. Pruitt, received a bayonet wound in the hip. Dr. Ewing says he has broken no bones and should be well within a few weeks, but he must be careful not to let infection set in. Dr. Ewing is also treating General Houston for a battle wound. I saw the great general resting against a giant oak tree, his shattered ankle bound up in white linen. He was writing someone a letter. The Mexicans shot two horses from beneath him, but the good Lord preserved our leader's precious life.

The marshes are full of Mexican corpses. How will they ever bury so many? The stench of rotting flesh makes the air all but unbearable to breathe. There are so many dead. How many are captured, I wonder? How many escaped into the swamp?

Father gave Sister and me permission to go see Santa Anna. Everyone wants to see that man who calls himself the Napoleon of the West. But I'm not going. I know several of the young men in the army who might be holding the prisoners. I do not want them to see me with a tablecloth covering my head! Not to mention that my dress is filthy, pinned up the back, my shoes down at the heels, and my stockings torn and splattered with mud. Sister and Priscilla are still deciding whether or not they're going.

Later

Guy is here on the San Jacinto battlefield! After seeing his family safely across the San Jacinto River, he turned back and enlisted as an orderly for Lieutenant

159

Colonel Somervell in the Texian army. He wasn't wounded in battle, but is terribly sick with the measles, as are so many of our soldiers.

The steamboat, the *Laura*, just arrived from Galveston bringing the first Texas government officials. When the *Laura* departs, Angus, Mother, Father, Sister, Priscilla, Mr. Pruitt, Little Henrietta and Domino, my baby brother, and I will be on board. It will carry us first to Galveston, then on to Velasco and up the Brazos to Wood's Landing. Uncle Peter, Aunty Rachel, Milindy, Flo, and Toby will return home overland with the stock and wagon. However, they must take a roundabout route part of the way there, because the Texians burned Vince's Bridge across Sims Bayou to prevent Mexican reinforcements from reaching Santa Anna.

Tuesday, April 26, 1836

On the San Jacinto Battlefield

Today is the anniversary of my birth. I am fifteen years old.

Father has named my new baby brother. He is to be called Samuel Houston Wood, after the man who saved Texas. What a brave man the General is. They say that even Santa Anna is in awe of his courage. He never imagined that General Houston would lead the charge at San Jacinto himself, placing his own life in mortal danger.

Tuesday, May 10, 1836

On board the Laura

Guess what distinguished passengers I am sailing with? None other than President Burnet, his cabinet ministers, and their infamous prisoner, Santa Anna! They're sailing with us as far as Velasco. There they will disembark to sign a treaty in which Mexico promises to stop warring against Texas and to recognize our independence. General Santa Anna has already ordered his second in command, General Filisola, to evacuate the rest of his troops from Texas and fall back to Monterrey.

General Houston is not on board. Evidently, his ankle wound is worse than they had thought. Dr. Ewing is sending him to New Orleans for an immediate operation.

Maggie and her family came aboard in Galveston. We fairly flew into each other's arms. Since then, though, she and I haven't had a moment to ourselves. Angus simply refuses to leave her side!

I said that Maggie was my best friend, but maybe I

have two best friends now. I couldn't have made it through this without Priscilla.

From other passengers, we are hearing horror stories of the destruction left by the Mexican army. Houses across Texas are ransacked, burned, destroyed. Cattle and goods are stolen. We're all worried sick what we might find at Wood's Landing—but not Mother. She is positively tranquil. "If we can have peace and we can have preaching," she said, "I won't care what property is gone."

Guy had to stay back in camp because he's gotten even sicker. Mother says I mustn't worry, that Dr. Ewing will give him the best of care. I don't know how he learned I was at San Jacinto, but, before I sailed, I received a garland of glossy green wild peach leaves. Attached was a card that said:

> *To Miss Belle Wood of Columbia:*
> *These are your victory laurels. Happy Birthday.*
> *Thine.*
> *Guy.*

Sunday, May 15, 1836

Home, Sweet Home

We arrived at our house to find everything still standing—and in the most glorious confusion! Even with the mess, it's pure joy to see my home again. The first thing we saw was the hogs running out the front door. Inside, we found Father's bookcase lying on the floor, broken open, his books, pipes, and papers scattered everywhere, and the hogs sleeping on them. The hens were cackling. Everywhere—in closets, on beds, atop bureaus—is a nest. The house is chock-full of eggs.

The Mexicans set a hot skillet on top of our mahogany bureau and left an ugly scorch mark. After killing our hogs, they cut them up on our fancy oak dining table, leaving deep gouges in the fine wood.

There was so much to do, but first we needed to eat. As Aunty Rachel and Milindy aren't here yet, we girls made the lunch. Afterwards, Father wiped his mouth with a napkin, excused himself from the table, and headed straight for the cornfield. He began plowing at once—on the Sabbath! He says the Lord would not suffer gladly a man who'd let his family starve, Sabbath or no. Father's not even waiting for Uncle Peter to get here to help. "We've no time to waste," he said on his way out the door, "if we want to eat this summer." With our fences down, the cattle and hogs that remained here broke into the fields and ate or trampled most of our corn crop. The field is full of weeds. Father must try to save whatever crop he can.

We've invited Priscilla, Flo, and Mr. Pruitt to lodge with us for a time. After we washed the dishes and Priscilla made her father comfortable, she, Sister, and I went out to hunt up the goods we had hidden away in the days before we left.

First, we went down to the river bottom to retrieve our crockery. But the Mexicans had been there ahead of us. Every dish we'd buried had been dug up and smashed to bits. Now what was the point of that? It just infuriates me.

Next, we visited the spot where Uncle Peter had buried the bushels of potatoes, vegetables, and corn midway between two posts. We could see that the Mexicans had pulled out the posts and dug holes around them. But they didn't think to dig in between the posts. They didn't find our stash. Outwitting the thieves gave me great satisfaction. How desperately we need that food. Tomorrow, I'll hitch up Beauty and we'll drive the cart back down there. We'll haul those provisions back to the storage mounds and cribs near the garden.

Last of all, we climbed the bluff to visit the cemetery, where we'd buried our books and other valuables. To our amazement, we found nothing had been disturbed. Nobody had even been digging up there. Everything was mud-encrusted but otherwise exactly as we had left it—even my silver mirror was intact.

We went back to the Big House to report to Mother. We found her in the kitchen, sitting shivering in a sudsy washtub. Little Henrietta was sitting on a stool nearby, holding Baby Sammy. I was shocked to see Mother bathing on the Sabbath, but Aunty Rachel insisted it was necessary for her recovery.

I grabbed a sponge and began soaping Mother's goose-bumpy back. I was curious about something. "Mother," I asked, squeezing the sponge so that the warm water trickled down her pale back, "don't you think it's odd that the Mexicans didn't dig up our cemetery? It seems such an obvious place to bury treasures. Surely they would have thought of that."

Mother cupped her hands and dipped them into the water, then splashed her face. "Sweetheart," she said, looking back at me over her shoulder, "those Mexican soldiers would never have disturbed any graves, especially ones with crosses."

Hmmm. . . . How odd. The Mexican soldiers defile

my home and kill my brother but respect a Christian burial ground.

Tonight my bedtime prayers seemed to stretch on forever. I've so much to be thankful for. Our cattle, hogs, and hens didn't run away. Our creeks and rivers are stocked with fish. Because of all the spring rain, wildflowers of every color blanket the prairie and dewberry bushes droop with fat fruit. Elms, oaks, and sycamores hum with birdsong. The Gulf breeze blows fresh and clean through my window, ruffling my curtains.

It seems wrong to be so happy after so much loss and suffering. How I long to bring back Mac and GM. But some things cannot be undone. Our own suffering has ended. We're saved, and Texas is saved. Amen.

Friday, August 19, 1836

I can't believe I haven't written a line here in three months. We've worked morning, noon, and night—every one of us—to get Wood's Landing back in shape. I've just been too tired at the end of the day to write about it.

It's not as if I haven't been writing, though. Almost every day I've written a letter to Guy. He's been through so much. His measles went into pneumonia, and he suffered a complete collapse. He's still recovering. Mrs. Perry has invited me to sail down to Peach Point at the end of this month. It's hard to believe that it's been five months since I've seen Guy. I can't wait.

So much has happened this warm and baking summer.

Almost all the Mexican soldiers have withdrawn, but one in particular remains—Santa Anna. We don't know what to do with him. Many Texians want to slip a noose around Santa Anna's neck, but General Houston won't have it. Texas must be a responsible nation. If Santa Anna is hanged, Father explained, the Americans will never allow us to become a state, which is what General Houston wants. Yet, how can we risk letting Santa Anna return to Mexico? Can he truly be trusted to honor the treaty he signed? Do the Americans not understand our dilemma? The debate rages on. So, for now, "El Presidente" remains our prisoner.

For most of June and July, Santa Anna was held at the Patton Plantation, just two miles northwest of here. We were curious to see him, so, in mid-July, a group of ladies from Columbia—Mother, Sister, Priscilla, and I included—rode out to the Patton place. When we arrived, Captain—now Major—Patton escorted us out to a wooden cabin behind his Big House to meet his most distinguished guest. There we found Santa Anna playing checkers with his Texas guards. Upon seeing us, he jumped out of his chair and rushed over to greet us cordially. He turned on his famous charm, kissing our outstretched hands, and toasting us with a little wine. He's much shorter than I expected, with curly, dark hair and fair skin.

Just days after our visit, we learned he had almost escaped. A beautiful Spanish lady paid him a visit, bearing candies and fine wine. As she was leaving, she let a small note, written on tissue paper, fall at his feet. Major Patton intercepted this note before Santa Anna could grab it and read it to himself. The note was written in Spanish. Not able to read Spanish, Major Patton left the room with the note to look for a translator.

The note revealed the escape plot. The lady was a Mexican spy. She had poisoned one of the wine bottles she had given to Santa Anna. In the note, she instructed Santa Anna to give the poisoned wine to his Texas guards. Once the guards were eliminated, she wrote, Santa Anna could escape on a horse she'd left waiting for him in the woods.

Meanwhile, as Major Patton was having this note translated, Santa Anna uncorked one of the bottles of poisoned wine and drank a glass. When Major Patton returned to Santa Anna's cabin, he found him dangerously ill. Major Patton placed him in the family carriage and rushed him to the Orozimbo Plantation to see Dr. Phelps. Dr. Phelps had to pump Santa Anna's stomach to save his life. Santa Anna was transferred to Orozimbo for security reasons. Just last week, though, he attempted another escape. Now he must wear a ball and chain attached to his leg.

As for General Houston, he almost died from his ankle wound, but now he's recovering nicely. I just love him. He's everybody's idol. Hands down, he'll be our next president, says Father.

Everyone up and down the Brazos is working to rebuild his property. Although most of our neighbors returned to their land after the exodus we call the Runaway Scrape, many did not. Take the Baron, for example. We think he's gone for good. The Mexicans burned his entire sugar plantation to the ground. Now that the Baron's gone, folks are saying he wasn't a real nobleman after all but a common criminal. They say that, besides smuggling slaves, he embezzled tax money in France and fled before he could be brought to trial. He was a complete fraud.

What a pity Moss doesn't know his former master is

gone. Guy writes that Moss is in Mexico. He was so sure he'd be captured by the Baron's bounty hunters that he left Texas with General Filisola's army.

John and Ann Thomas never returned to Bailey's Prairie. The red cottage sits empty once again. Maybe Mr. Thomas really did believe in the ghost after all and used the Mexicans as an excuse to get away from it!

Aunty Rachel has told me everything she knows about the ghost of Bailey's Prairie. He's the ghost of Brit Bailey, the original resident of the red cottage, who died in the cholera epidemic of '32. In his will, Mr. Bailey requested to be buried standing up, facing west, rifle at his side, with a jug of whiskey at his feet. In this way, he said, he would be standing, armed, and ready should an enemy approach. He had many enemies in life. But, upon his death, Mr. Bailey's widow was only willing to honor the first three requests of her late husband's will. She absolutely refused to lower a jug of whiskey in his grave. "He had enough of that stuff in life!" she exclaimed. (Mr. Bailey was a hard drinker.)

Now, on dark and rainy nights, Mr. Bailey's ghost is said to wander the prairie with his lantern, searching for more whiskey. When I see Guy, the first thing I am going to ask him is if he was carrying a lantern the night he rescued me on Bailey's Prairie. I hope he says yes. In the meanwhile, I have no reason to cross Bailey's Prairie ever again. Maggie married Angus and moved with him to his farm on Caney Creek. Her mother and the baby Patrick are living there, too.

Sister has not mentioned Capt. Ross since we've come home. She's too distracted by all the eligible young men back from the army.

Priscilla's father recovered from his wound and returned to Bolivar, but I persuaded her and Flo to stay with us for as long as they want. Priscilla's a perfect friend. Little Henrietta cannot imagine life without her. And Flo loves to help Mother with Baby Sammy, who's a handful.

Guy wrote to say that his stepfather wants to send him to the States to study law. Father, too, plans to enroll me in a school on the East Coast—perhaps as early as next spring. I do so want to be a teacher! So it looks as if, for the next few years, Guy and I might be living as far apart as two people can be. I won't be able to hop on a boat for Peach Point and he won't be able to jump on a horse and ride to Wood's Landing. I guess we'll have to make summers and holidays in Texas our special time for reunion.

I'm young. There's so much I want to see and do. I want to meet new people and explore new places. But no matter how far away my travels and studies may take me, one thing's for sure. I'll always come back to Texas, where my friends and family are. Texas will always be my home—my home, sweet home.

Author's Note

In 1835, when our story opens, Texas belonged to Mexico. Everyone living in Texas was, by law, a Mexican citizen. Back then, though, the term Mexicans was not generally used to refer to people living inside Texas. In general, it was used to refer to citizens of Mexico living outside Texas, and, specifically, to Mexican soldiers. People living in Texas were called Texians.

Our story—told in diary format—takes place in Stephen F. Austin's Colony, a settlement populated largely by Anglo planters from the Southern United States and their slaves. The diarist, the fictional character Belle Wood, belongs to one of these Anglo families. Characters in this story include enslaved African-American men, women, and children. Some are depicted experiencing better living conditions than are others. Although some plantation families did, like the Woods, look upon their slaves almost as extended family, it is not the intent of this book or its author to excuse or condone the practice of one human owning another under any condition.

Hispanic Texians, who call themselves Tejanos, settled two very important towns in our story, San Antonio de Béxar (called both San Antonio and Béxar) and La Bahía (renamed Goliad in 1829). Although all four of these place names were in use during the Texas Revolution, Belle calls the towns simply San Antonio and Goliad.

Remember the Alamo! is fiction, and the adventures of the Wood family and the other fictional characters are imaginary. But the story it tells of the Texas Revolution is faithful to the historical record. The actions and words of the real people in this drama are either historical or historically consistent with their recorded words and deeds. No work of this nature can be free of controversy or error, but, as you will see, I have tried to give a true and full picture of a most incredible period in the history of a most incredible state, the glorious state of Texas.

LWR

Life in Austin's Colony, Texas

1835–1836

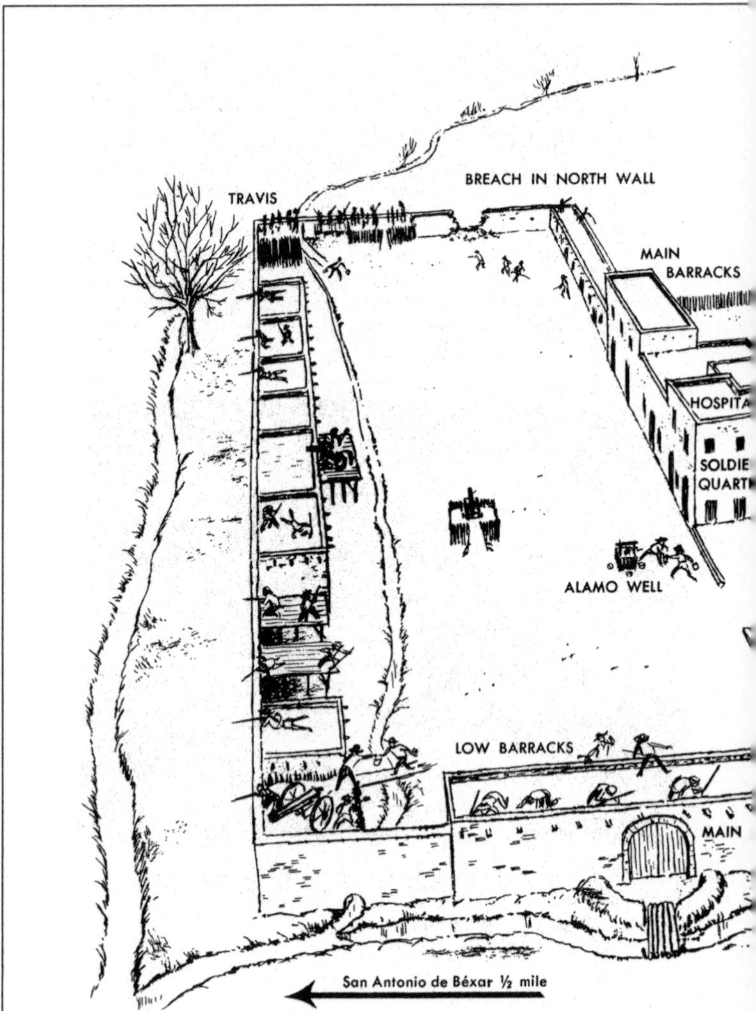

TRAVIS
BREACH IN NORTH WALL
MAIN BARRACKS
HOSPITA
SOLDIE QUART
ALAMO WELL
LOW BARRACKS
MAIN
San Antonio de Béxar ½ mile

The Alamo Under Fire reprinted from *13 Days to Glory* by Lon Tinkle, by permission of the Texas A&M Press.

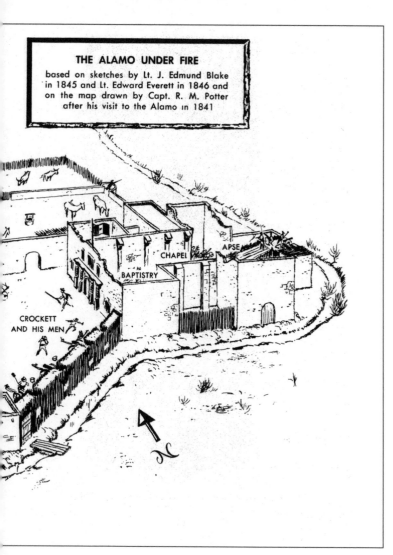

THE ALAMO UNDER FIRE

based on sketches by Lt. J. Edmund Blake in 1845 and Lt. Edward Everett in 1846 and on the map drawn by Capt. R. M. Potter after his visit to the Alamo in 1841

CHAPEL

APSE

BAPTISTRY

CROCKETT AND HIS MEN

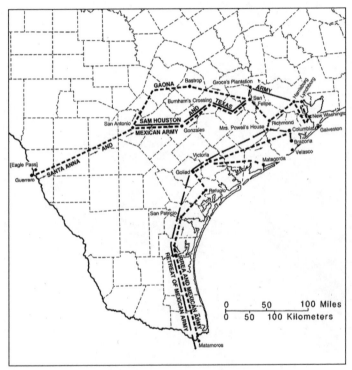

"The Texas Revolution" modified and reprinted from *Historical Atlas of Texas* by A. Ray Stephens and William M. Holmes, by permission of University of Oklahoma Press.

The Runaway Scrape

In January of 1836, Mexican General Antonio López de Santa Anna crossed the Rio Grande with six thousand troops. His target was San Antonio and the Texian troops occupying it. It seemed an odd choice. Only 150 volunteers defended the fort there called the Alamo. Such a small army posed no real military threat to Santa Anna.

Strategically, Presidio La Bahía (Goliad) would have been a better choice. Five hundred rebels under the command of Col. James Fannin defended that fort. Also, Goliad sat on the Atascosito Road that led into East Texas. That made Goliad the door to Anglo Texas—a hotbed of rebellion. If Santa Anna wanted to crush the Texas revolution, Goliad was the key.

But Santa Anna was an impulsive man. He was out for revenge. He had not forgotten the humiliation

General Cós suffered when defeated at San Antonio in December. Santa Anna wanted San Antonio badly. He planned to wipe out the Alamo men and make them a bloody example to the rest of the Texas rebels.

On February 23, Santa Anna's army arrived in San Antonio, a month before they were expected. For thirteen days, the Mexicans pelted the Alamo with cannon fire and rifle shot, but the Texians held the fort. Finally, in the gray, predawn hours of March 6, the Mexicans stormed the fort, overwhelming the Texians with sheer numbers. Every Alamo defender was slaughtered. The lives of some thirty noncombatants—women, children, and blacks—were spared.

Santa Anna sent one of the survivors, Susanna Dickinson, to deliver the news of the fall of the Alamo to General Sam Houston, who was headquartered at Gonzales. Upon receiving this message, General Houston also learned that the Mexican army was advancing rapidly toward Gonzales. With a command of only 374 soldiers, he decided to make a hasty retreat until he could gather a larger fighting force and make a decent stand against Santa Anna's thousands.

As the news spread of the fall of the Alamo and Santa Anna's murderous rampage across the countryside, panic ensued. Texas roads were soon clogged with

Susanna Dickinson, H. B. Hillyer, c. 1875, reprinted by permission of the Texas State Library and Archives Commission. Susanna Dickinson was in the Alamo with her baby when the Alamo fell. Santa Anna spared her life so she could carry a warning to General Houston: anyone who defied him would die. When the Texians learned that the Mexican army was on the move again, they panicked. Everyone either fought or fled in the mass exodus that came to be known as the Runaway Scrape.

The Runaway Scrape reprinted from *Plantation Life in Texas* by Elizabeth Silverthorne, by permission of the Texas A&M University Press. After the colonists learned of the fall of the Alamo and the advance of Santa Anna's troops, panic set in. Some families fled their homes within an hour of hearing the news, with their tables spread for the daily meal. Every road leading eastward out of Texas was crowded with the throng of moving people, running from the Mexican army. Backwards and forwards, as far as the eye could see, stretched a moving mass of animals and human beings, walking, riding, and in every kind of vehicle.

settlers frantically fleeing their homes in a flight now referred to as the Runaway Scrape.

At that time, Dilue Rose Harris was a child of ten, living with her family at Stafford's Point in Austin's Colony. She remembered the day the courier brought the letter from General Houston urging them to flee their homes at once:

> We left home at sunset, hauling clothes, bedding, and provisions on the sleigh with one yoke of oxen. Mother and I were walking, she with an infant in her arms. Brother drove the oxen, and my two little sisters rode in the sleigh.

It was a cold and rainy spring. The journey was a nightmare of terror and suffering:

> Our hardships began at the Trinity. The river was rising and there was a struggle to see who should cross first. Measles, sore eyes, whooping cough, and every other disease that man, woman, or child is heir to, broke out among us. . . . The horrors of crossing the Trinity are beyond my power to describe. One of my sisters was very sick, and the ferryman said that those families with sick children should cross first.

When our party got to the boat the water broke over the banks above where we were and ran around us. We were several hours surrounded by water. Our family was the last to get to the boat. . . . The sick child was in convulsions. It required eight men to manage the boat.

Five days later, Dilue's sister died. She was buried in the cemetery at Liberty. A few days later, the Harrises received more bad news: Fannin and his Goliad men had been massacred.

The Harris family had been at Liberty three weeks when, one Thursday evening, they heard a sound like distant thunder. Dilue's father said it was cannon fire from a battle. Sure that the Texians had been defeated and the Mexicans were on the move eastward again, the Harris family set out for the safety of the U.S. border.

A little way down the road, they heard some shouting coming up behind them. They turned to see a young man on horseback riding up toward them, waving his hat, and yelling, "Turn back! The Texas army has whipped the Mexican army and the Mexican army are prisoners! Turn back!" The Texas army had defeated the Mexicans at San Jacinto in a battle had lasted only eighteen minutes. The Texians had charged into battle crying, "Remember the Alamo! Remember Goliad!"

The Surrender of Santa Anna by William Henry Huddle, reprinted by permission of Texas State Library and Archives Commission. In this commemorative painting, Mexican General Antonio López de Santa Anna stands before the wounded General Sam Houston. This surrender took place on April 22, 1836, the day after the Battle of San Jacinto. Santa Anna's capture cemented Texas independence, which had been declared by a convention fifty-one days earlier at Washington-on-the-Brazos.

The martyrdom of the Texian defenders at the Alamo and at Goliad had provided the Texians at San Jacinto with a mighty battle cry that swept them to a glorious and decisive victory, giving birth to the new and grand Republic of Texas.

The Steamer Yellow Stone *on the 19th April 1833* by Carl Bodmer, reprinted by permission of the Joslyn Art Museum, Omaha, Nebraska. The steamship, the *Yellow Stone,* under the command of Capt. John E. Ross, was loading cotton above San Felipe when Sam Houston's army arrived on March 31, 1836, in a heavy rainstorm. The Texians were forced to encamp on the west side of the Brazos River because its flooding prevented their crossing. But they could not delay; Santa Anna's army was in hot pursuit. Capt. John Ross commanded his crew to ferry the Texas army across the swollen river. General Houston later praised the *Yellow Stone* for helping him overtake the enemy and "save Texas."

Man on Horseback by W. G. M. Samuels, reprinted by permission of the Alamo. Horses were indispensable in the Texas Revolution. When Stephen F. Austin issued the call-to-arms, Texian men grabbed their guns, saddled up their horses, and rode off to join the army. The women were left at home to defend themselves, many without transportation.

187

A Typical Texas

Down Home reprinted from *Plantation Life in Texas* by Elizabeth Silverthorne, by permission of the Texas A&M University Press.

The offer of cheap and fertile land drew many planters from the Southern United States to settle in Texas—and, in particular, to Austin's Colony, where timber and water were in great abundance. Many of these Southern planters established large plantations much like the ones they had left behind—run on slave labor.

The typical Texas plantation was largely self-sufficient, except for books, fine cloth, furniture, and staples such as coffee, flour, and salt.

Plantation

A. The "Big House"—home to the planter family

B. kitchen

C. vegetable, herb, and flower garden

D. field planted in a cash crop such as cotton

E. slave quarters

F. carriage house

G. blacksmith shop

H. barn & stock pens

I. cotton gin

J. riverboat landing

K. slave overseer's home

L. family cemetery

The Pioneer Cowpen by Friedrich Richard Petri, c. 1853, reprinted by permission of Janet Long Fish. Texas pioneers were not always rich plantation owners. Many immigrants, like the Petri-Lungwitz family from Germany shown here, did not own slaves but worked their own small farms.

Sugar Harvest in Louisiana and Texas, Franz Holzlhuber, 1856–60. Collection of Glenbow Museum, Calgary, Canada. By 1840, cotton was still king but most of the planters on the Colorado and Brazos Rivers grew a few patches of sugar cane. To run a commercial sugar plantation, however, required a huge work force—of Negro slaves. The harvest and production of sugar and syrup required the time and attention of many slaves. Each fall, before the first frost was expected, slaves cut the cane and stripped them of leaves. The cane then had to be ground within a few hours of cutting. During corn-grinding season, slaves had to work eighteen-hour days.

$50 REWARD.

RUNAWAY from the subscriber, on the 22nd ultimore, a Negro Man named

ANDREW;

Twenty-two years of age, well made, not very dark, about five feet ten or eleven inches high, a scar on the back of his neck, occasioned by a burn—He sometimes stammers a little when spoken to. It is believed the above named negro has been enticed off by some white man. The above reward will be given for the apprehension of the thief and negro, or twenty dollars for the negro alone, delivered to me at the Walnut Hills, or secured in any jail so I get him again.

JOEL CAMERON.

Walnut Hills, Oct. 22nd, 1824—127-3t*

Advertisement for runaway slave Andrew, reprinted from the *Mississippian and Natchez Adviser,* October 22, 1824, by permission of the Center for American History, University of Texas–Austin. Slaves dealt with their servitude in different ways. Some felt well-treated and remained loyal. Others, though, hated their situations and rebelled, usually by running away. If caught, runaways paid a high price. Slave patrols roved the woods with attack dogs. The punishment for a fugitive's first offense was thirty-nine lashes with a rawhide whip called the "black snake." Thousands of slaves did successfully escape to Mexico where "they didn't care what color you were, black, white, yellow, or blue," recalled former slave Felix Haywood.

192

"Miss Frances L. (Judith) Trask," from *The Texas Republic* by William Ransom Hogan, reprinted by permission of the Center for American History, University of Texas–Austin. In early Texas, there was no public education system. Mothers often taught their children or families joined together to employ teachers who lived in their patrons' homes and took their pay in produce. Books were scarce. Weather, crops, Indians, and the threat of war regulated the length of the school terms. The first boarding school for girls was opened in Coles Settlement in 1835 by the stylish Frances L. Trask of Gloucester, Massachusetts, who wrote to her father that her "school was small but profitable, as tuition is high, from $6.00 to $10.00 per quarter."

The Equestrian Portrait of Sam Houston by Stephen Seymour Thomas, 1893, reprinted by permission of the San Jacinto Museum of History. General Sam Houston was the commmander of the Texas army. He led his troops into battle and a stunning victory.

About Lisa Waller Rogers

There's nothing like a good old Texas ghost story—and the one about Bailey's Light remains one of the best. "When doing research for my first book, *A Texas Sampler*, I kept running across stories about a character named Brit Bailey," said Ms. Rogers. "He was a wild man! Some people said he had been a pirate with Jean Lafitte at Galveston. He loved to fight. Once he arrived home to find Stephen F. Austin courting his daughter. Mr. Bailey ran Mr. Austin off his land, shooting at his boots as he scooted down the lane."

Ann Raney Thompson Coleman, writing of her life in early Texas, agreed that Mr. Bailey was a rough character. "[He] was much addicted to drinking spirituous liquors and was insane during these times. In one of his drinking fits, he set fire to all his out houses, barn, and stables." It was only through the pleading of his daughter that Mr. Bailey spared their dwelling house from going up in flames.

If anyone would know the character of Brit Bailey, that person would be Ann. She knew him well in life and—maybe—in death. Upon her arrival in Austin's Colony, Ann Raney and her father lodged with Mr. Bailey at his house seven miles from Brazoria. When Ann married her first husband, John Thomas, in 1833, Mr. Bailey's daughter served as her bridesmaid. After Mr. Bailey died and his family moved elsewhere, Ann and John bought the old Bailey plantation.

Ann knew something was wrong with their new home the day they moved in. "On arriving there, every one of us was tired and thirsty. I took a survey of the place, which had a wild and gloomy appearance, such as you often read of in enchanted places. The dwelling house was painted red, a kitchen smoke house and some outbuildings; a pecan orchard about a quarter of a mile long led like an avenue up to the house, having to cross a big pond of water before entering the grove. . . . In the grove close to the house was the grave of Mr. Bailey. . . . It was about as large around as a wash tub bottom." Mr. Bailey was buried standing on his feet, shotgun at his side.

Although Ann was convinced of the essential evilness of the spot, she and her family moved in. If you've just finished reading this book, you know what happened next. After the fall of the Alamo, the Thomas family abandoned the old Bailey place and fled during the Runaway Scrape, settling in Louisiana.

In the years that followed, there was whispered talk among the local residents of something luminous moving about in the pecan grove on Bailey's Prairie. It was reported that the ghost sometimes shot out of the earth as a column of light as big as a man, frightening dogs so badly they crawled home on their bellies whimpering. Other times, the apparition appeared as a great ball of fire bouncing and rolling across the prairie, darting in and out among the trees before finally shooting up into the sky and disappearing.

Sightings of Bailey's Light continue until the present day. It is said that on dark and rainy nights, especially in the late fall or early winter, near the spot where Brit Bailey was buried, there can frequently be seen a white figure moving back and forth in the trees, swinging a lantern, looking, always looking, for something.

Old-timers say that, if by some chance if you happen to be out on Bailey's Prairie on such a night, it is advisable that you travel through at maximum speed. You never know what might be waiting for you there.

When Lisa Waller Rogers writes a history book, she

wants it to be accurate as well as entertaining. She spends months in libraries gathering information young readers will find interesting. She reads old diaries, letters, newspaper articles, and journal entries written by real people who lived long ago. She discovers what they ate, read, wore, and did for fun. "History should capture the flavor of the times, not just the facts," she is fond of saying.

Ms. Rogers's first history, *A Texas Sampler: Historical Recollections,* was a finalist for the Texas Institute of Letters Best Book for Children/Young People Award. Her second book, *Angel of the Alamo,* received wide acclaim for its beautiful illustrations and Ms. Rogers's "obvious gift for storytelling," wrote Judyth Rigler in the San Antonio Express-News (June 4, 2000). Book 1 in her Lone Star Journal series, *Get Along, Little Dogies: The Chisholm Trail Diary of Hallie Lou Wells,* has been called "the ultimate Wild West adventure" (*Texas Books in Review,* Spring 2001) and is a 2003–2004 Lamplighter Award finalist. Book 2, *The Great Storm: The Hurricane Diary of J. T. King,* won the 2002 Western Heritage Award for Outstanding Juvenile Book. In reviewing *The Great Storm,* Deborah Wormser of the *Dallas Morning News* praises Rogers as "a true storyteller who handles both the drama and the horror with grace," concluding that Rogers's "research and her ear for dialogue . . . carry the day."

Ms. Rogers is a sixth-generation Texan. She lives in Austin with her husband, Tom, their daughter, Katie, and four dachshunds: Fargo, Emma, Cookie, and Sammy Tomato.